FLEA CIRCUS
A BRIEF BESTIARY OF GRIEF

A NOVEL

MANDY KEIFETZ

New Issues Poetry & Prose

Western Michigan University
Kalamazoo, Michigan 49008

First Edition, 2012.

ISBN: 978-1-936970-04-9

Library of Congress Cataloging-in-Publication Data:
Keifetz, Mandy
Flea Circus: a brief bestiary of grief/Mandy Keifetz
Library of Congress Control Number: 2011927814

Cover Design: Margaret Wolicki
Production Manager: Paul Sizer
The Design Center, Gwen Frostic School of Art
College of Fine Arts
Western Michigan University

This book is the winner of the Association of Writers & Writing Programs (AWP)
Award for the Novel. AWP is a national, nonprofit organization dedicated to
serving American letters, writers, and programs of writing.
Go to www.awpwriter.org for more information.

FLEA CIRCUS

A BRIEF BESTIARY OF GRIEF

A NOVEL

MANDY KEIFETZ

NEW ISSUES

 WESTERN MICHIGAN UNIVERSITY

This book is for Dex, Sophie Athena and Arlo. They are the finest family any girl could want.

Humanity is faced with a double perspective: in one direction, violent pleasure, horror and death —precisely the perspective of poetry—and in the opposite direction, that of science or the real world of utility. Only the useful, the real, have a serious character. We are never within our rights in preferring seduction. Truth has rights over us. Indeed, it has every right. And yet we can, and indeed we must, respond to something which, not being God, is stronger than every right, that impossible to which we accede only by forgetting the truth of all these rights, only by accepting disappearance.

—Georges Bataille

1. ALTAMONT

Abeyance ◆ Airshaft ◆ Alcohol ◆ Alias ◆ Alive ◆ Altamont ◆
Animal Enthusiast ◆ Antimonial Lead ◆ Ash Bat ◆ Audio Frequency ◆ Awful

A is for Altamont.

Not because you died at the Speedway Free Festival. You were only six years old during the End of Innocence, safely tucked in your Brooklyn bed, too little and too far away to be squashed in a panicked crowd, or drowned in an irrigation canal. Too young to be knifed by a meth addict or beaten to a pulp by Hell's Angels, hired for security.

A is for Altamont, but not because you died at the festival. Not because the events herein described took place there. God knows we're too young for that. You were nine. I wouldn't be born for eight years. 1969 was forty-two years ago.

And God help me if that long ago from now I'm still alive. I'm aiming myself, steadily, certainly, at that final vault, and if I should chance upon a hyped-up security guard interested in helping me along, don't think I won't leap at the chance.

You did.

Leap at the chance, I mean.

You poor bastard, Tim, way too young to have died at Altamont.

But dead anyway.

No, we'll give A over to Altamont because that is the name of the cat you left in my charge. I'm looking at him now; looking at him looking at the boarded-up back window as if he can see through it. I like to think he can, like to think he can see through all the layers of medium-density fiberboard and sheetrock and muslin to the airshaft as it was before you lay crumpled there, before we moved in here together, before your sour old granny was a gleam in her daddy's eye.

Altamont is brown and fat like a coconut, and riddled with fleas, but not cat fleas. Oh, no. Not Altamont. Not cat fleas. Hedgehog fleas. *Archaeopsylla erinacei,* you used to call them. He's riddled with them because I can't bear to give him a dip yet, which is not the squeamish way it seems, exactly.

He's got the crossed faraway eyes of an unattainable woman. I like to think he's looking at the airshaft as it was in the middle of someone *else's* tragedy. I like to think of him in the 1880s, the apartment's first cat, staring out there and seeing some wretched fool, a leech breeder, maybe, or a club tout, dancing away from slop pails as their contents pour from windows, out of his mind (the leech-breeder, not Altamont) on benzene-needled beer. I like to think of Altamont that way, and then again I don't.

Altamont isn't all there anymore and I'm worried about him. I keep swearing I'll change his name to trick the angel of death, but thinking of a new name is too hard. Nights pass into mornings in a blur of stale alcohol and television and I find that I've called him Altamont again.

It always struck me as sentimental to name a cat Altamont. And sentiment, since you died, no longer interests me. But neither can I gather the will to think up a new name.

At five o'clock this morning, Altamont and I watched a television report on High-Rise Cat Syndrome. Did you know about High-Rise Cat Syndrome when you were alive, Tim?

See, if you pitch a cat out of a tenement window—say a four-story job, say one on Howard Street, say the one you pitched yourself out of, say the one I'm staring through now, even though it's covered with layers of sheetrock and medium-density fiberboard and muslin—if you pitch a cat out a tenement window, chances are you'll end up with a cat pancake.

A falling body accelerates at a rate of 32.2 feet per second per second. Same as it was in 1598 when Galileo first struggled his gouty ass up to the top of the Tower of Pisa to drop shit off and count. The rate of acceleration of a falling body, any body, a cat's brown furry body, or a hollow-bodied Gibson ES-355, such as Keith Richards played at Altamont.

Gravity doesn't care what's falling. Any falling body accelerates at a rate of 32.2 feet per second per second. If you toss a live cat out a tenement window, chances are you'll end up with a cat pancake.

If, on the other hand, a cat gets tossed off a high-rise roof, and therefore has time to tumble through the air and get his feet under him, the worst he's likely to suffer is a split palate when his little head bounces against the concrete. No kidding. Same standard gravity, same rate of acceleration, but the extra time still makes a difference for live cats. Scientists who study such things (whoever *they* are) have recently announced this.

Deranged animal enthusiasts, the kind of sentimentalists who believe that people begin, over time, to take on the characteristics of their pets, the kind of sentimentalists who name their cats for the End of Innocence—the kind of sentimentalist you were, Tim— have a lot of problems with this theory. They question, reasonably enough, I suppose, just how the unnamed scientists came to their conclusion. You can't help but picture white-clad eggheads gleefully tossing kittens off roofs, listening for the concrete thud. And getting paid for it.

I myself don't care for cats anymore and if such a job were available, I'd probably take it on as a sideline; but I'm a sensible girl, I always was, and I tend to suspect that the discovery of High-Rise Cat Syndrome was based largely on anecdotal evidence.

Someone went around to veterinary clinics, animal hospitals and shelters, interviewed pets and their owners, found out how high up they lived, etc. Maybe a cat or two got tossed, just so they could get the stop-motion footage of the little bastard getting his feet under him as he tumbled. That would be no great loss to me. Sentiment, as I say, no longer interests me.

Anyhow, if it's true that cats are less likely to survive a short fall, say from your standard tenement window, then it's probably also true that pets rub their charming little habits off on their owners. What worries me for Altamont, of course, is the converse.

Altamont is the color of a corroded battery. He bats at flies, will play catch with a wadded-up cigarette box and begs like a dog if ham is being served. Late at night, when he howls at all the wild toms through the boarded-up window in the back room, he sounds like a girl laughing at a cocktail party.

What would you call a cat like that if you needed to trick the angel of death? Something with an A for Alias, so he won't get confused. Aqua Tint? Audio Frequency? Antimonial Lead? Well, not you. I know what you'd call a cat like that, you son of a bitch. You'd call him Altamont.

I remember the christening because you adopted us on the same day. I suppose I shouldn't say that because we were lovers, *equal partners*, as the women's magazines say.

People keep leaving women's magazines for me, Tim. I don't know what I'm supposed to do with them. I pile them up in the corner. Maybe I'm building you a cairn. I look at the glossy mountain they've become and think, what's with this? Are they meant to assuage my grief, or what? Am I supposed to use them as sponges for my sorrow? Mine them for tips on fixing myself up so

I can snag another guy? I don't know.

I always relied on you to tell me what the hell people were thinking. The world is never the way I think it is, and I can't understand my well-meaning benefactors anymore than I could ever understand the sensibility of women's magazines. But I suppose I'll have to try.

I suppose I shouldn't say that you adopted me and Altamont on the same day because to say so seems creepy. Because to say so would upset the people leaving women's magazines for me. Because we were lovers.

Nevertheless, I used to sit on my fire escape in the late afternoons, watching you watching the kids play in the mud and alley cat shit at the base of the airshaft. Watching you watching me watching the kids. Watching the kids watching us flirt by watching them.

The architectural idea of our building was to cram as many humans in as possible, and to provide them with the barest minimum of light and air—and a place to empty slop pails. The space between the buildings was not designed for cats to roam in, nor indeed for kids to play in. But cats and kids and their diseases have ruled these airshafts and "courtyards" since the first such tenement and likely always will.

Did you ever wonder why my side of the airshaft had a fire escape? Wonder about that flash of sheer engineering stupidity? Wonder where the hell someone from my side of the building was supposed to go after climbing down the fire escape, her world in flames, the airshaft totally walled in, except for a fire escape leading back up to a fire? Did you ever think that if we'd moved into my apartment instead of yours, you'd've had to leap out onto Howard Street because the fire escape would've been in your way?

In any event, our flirting was progressing quite nicely on

the afternoon you adopted Altamont. We'd established, shouting across the airshaft, playfully, that most of the people in the building, the adults at least, were insane. I don't think either of us were excepting ourselves, but maybe that doesn't matter.

We used to kid around about how the various loons in the building were at war with one another, competing for a title, most bughouse of them all. In our imagined airshaft, the edges filed off, the tenants of 33 Howard Street were deeply suspicious of one another. The greatest loathing, we determined, being between Mrs. Miles, the Cat Lady, and the tenant in 4-R, our resident foster father, who was the legal caretaker of the moment of most of the kids playing beneath us and who insisted that everyone address him as Uncle Willy.

Mrs. Miles' monomania, an obsession with "rescuing" alley cats, was in fact kind of low-rent when compared with Uncle Willy's elaborate flight of personal fancy, namely that he could save every unwanted, unlovely Keane-eyed brat who passed through his hands. But you thought that in the final analysis, Mrs. Miles was more insane because she imagined she was helping the cats, when in fact she was doing them grave harm.

Grave harm. I've been saying that to myself a lot lately. I look in the mirror and intone it. I brush my teeth to the tune of it. Like anything repeated endlessly, it has begun to sound funny to me. Grave harm. It's a square dance maneuver. It's a plastic gardening implement. It's a Finnish meat traditionally served with cheese. It's a dirge.

I remember thinking that these schisms we'd invented were vaguely embarrassing if true. Shouldn't they all have belonged to some sort of club? I remember thinking to myself you were the craziest tenant of all. Because while Mrs. M. thought she could save alley cats and Uncle Willy thought he could save children, you thought you could save . . . well, no. Perhaps I'd better not say it.

I remember thinking to myself you were the craziest tenant of all because you, Tim Acree, wee Tim Acree, son of a dockside barkeep, shit-kicker, street kid, you'd pulled yourself up by your goddamn bootstraps, merchant-marined your way through college to become an entomologist, then threw it all away only to attempt to revive an art form/racket that was dead and good riddance long before you were born. I remember thinking you were the craziest tenant of all because you, Tim Acree, shit-kicker, street kid, called yourself Professor Aloysius on stage; because you, Tim Acree, were the unlikeliest fucking performance artist in the world.

Mrs. Miles was a matronly steel-haired woman given to puttering about at dusk in the airshaft. She had thick, veiny legs and always wore the same pale blue nightie with a fraying scalloped hem. Her apartment had long since reached critical cat mass. I mean, there was not room in there for even one more cat.

In fact, if she opened her door, which she did now and again to yell at me for making too much noise in the halls, a cat or two would shoot out and down the stairs. This always precipitated a great wailing from Mrs. Miles and meant she'd certainly be down in the airshaft that night, armed not only with her usual baking pans of stinking cat food, but also with a tattered net which she used to capture replacement cats.

Mrs. Miles of course had no money and after the kids had gone up to Uncle Willy's for dinner, but before she emerged for her night's huntin', you sometimes used to scale down the airshaft on your side like Spider-Man, climb the fire escape on my side and perch next to me in my iron aerie. We'd extinguish cigarettes in beer cans and speculate about just how she managed to feed not only the cats in her apartment, but also their comrades in the airshaft.

I first fell in love with you the day you shyly suggested that she ground up some of the cats to feed the others. I laughed and looked away because my heart was dancing in my chest. Damn my heart.

I was convinced at that moment I'd found a real ally. Me and you, across our lonely airshaft courtyard, against the world. Well, maybe not the world. But at least against Mrs. Miles.

It was certainly true that Mrs. Miles pitied and detested anyone who did not share her passion, which, fortunately for the cats, was everyone else. We liked to watch Uncle Willy's kids take a kind of fledgling scientific interest in them, tie their tails, race them in poster mailing tubes. But to Mrs. Miles this was even worse than ignoring them altogether.

On the afternoon you adopted Altamont, we were on our respective roosts, watching the kids play a vicious tackle version of capture-the-flag which they'd adapted especially for the tiny space allotted them. Probably the game was occasionally interrupted by a yowl-fest from the holes where the feral toms hid during daylight. The cats had grown fat and mean by this time, and their obscene numbers bolstered their courage.

But my ears were deaf to that almost constant music. I was giddy with my crush on you, pretending to be sullen, watching the bend in your long leg as you sat on your windowsill, imagining the salt in the crease there if only I could get my mouth on it.

Twice Mrs. Miles leaned out her window and yelled at the kids to shut up because they were disturbing the cats. This too was an interruption that I'd grown immune to. The shrill, demented shouts from the windows that surrounded the airshaft constituted a barrage of sorts. I only had ears for you.

The third time the Cat Lady struggled open her window she poured an entire bucket of hot water onto the kids. No one was really hurt, although Fuz, Uncle Willy's oldest ward, who was in the blue team's jail right under Mrs. Miles's window and took the game much too seriously to jump away, even in case of natural disaster, swallowed a little of the water and threw up.

Our eyes met, and moments later we were side by side, banging on the Cat Lady's door, getting our first full-length upright view of one another. My God, how you looked, Tim. Long yellow supple, you looked like a good ash bat.

Mrs. Miles opened the door. Two cats shot through my legs and down the stairs past us. I started coughing as Mrs. Miles wedged herself in the doorframe in such a way as to prevent any further escapes. The smell of the Cat Lady's apartment was unbelievable.

"Whaddaya want?" she said and Tim, eerily formal under duress, you gave a little bow.

"Am I crazy, Ma'am," you said and I had to stifle a laugh, "or did I just see you empty a bucket of hot water on a bunch of kids?"

"Yeah. And so what? I got them brats good. Got was comin' to 'em. Bad boys, teasing my cats."

"Are you suggesting that you have doused the children in retaliation for the noise they made while playing, which noise in turn disturbed your animals?"

You whirled and looked at me when I said that and I admit it sounded strange, but it's not like I was a brain or anything. I was taking my cues from you, the little bow and all.

"I ain't suggestin' nothin', you little tramp. You got somethin' to say, say it."

Your jaw set then, like a movie star's, like something impervious—your jaw which would shatter upon impact.

"I've got something to say," you said.

"Yeah?"

"If you ever so much as look out your window at the kids again, I'll go down the airshaft and poison all the cats."

The Cat Lady's face shriveled up in terror and disgust. It

took several seconds, I think, for the full force of what you'd said to register with her. When it did, the effect was alarming. She seemed to shrink, and the fumes of cat-pee ammonia intensified. Her mouth, filled with rotten teeth, tightened, then opened in a perfect "o."

"Oh, you, you, you—you are a horrible man," she said.

"Yeah, Mrs. Miles. I'm a horrible man. I'm the man my life has made me. Just remember what I said. Don't bother those kids. Let them play in the goddamn airshaft. In fact, I think I'll start with this one."

And with that, you reached in behind the Cat Lady, scooped Altamont into my arms, and we headed back to your place.

"Anyway," you said, "I need him for the fleas."

A few days after your funeral, I was leaning out the back window and I overheard Uncle Willy whisper to the Cat Lady, "Her heart must be in the grave." He gestured vaguely toward our apartment, and looking up to find me leaning there, they scuttled away, embarrassed. It was after that that I boarded up the window with medium-density fiberboard and sheetrock and muslin.

My heart must be in the grave.

My first thought on hearing this of course was that my heart wasn't in the grave. It was in the goddamn airshaft. Later in the week though, I ran into Uncle Willy on the front stoop and he grabbed my wrist and said it again. Your heart must be in the grave.

"Very well," I said, "if it must, it must."

I'd been holding that line in abeyance, which A is also for, for years, but it came out of my mouth joyless. Well, of course it did. My heart is in the grave. My heart is directing my head in an awful, febrile direction.

The truth is that my heart, like my head, like a hyped-up Hell's Angels security guard, is sick. My heart doesn't know

12

wherefore my fucking mouth speaks. My heart thinks its only job is to care for your cat and your fleas, 'til they die too, then exit. My heart is doing grave harm. Inside me, my heart is staging its own private Altamont.

A is for Airshaft which I think I'll call your cat. Just to trick the angel of death, I mean.

2. BAR

Bacanora   Real   ◆   Balls   ◆   Balustrade   ◆   Bar   ◆   Blessed   ◆   Bluffing
Body   ◆   Bogeyman   ◆   Bohunk   gravitas   ◆   Boredom   ◆   Bottle   ◆   Bouncer
Breathless   ◆   Breathtaking   ◆   Brooklyn   House   of   D.   ◆   Brother   ◆   Bugging

B is for Bar. For the three weeks since you died, I've been working in your brother's bar, which used to be your father's bar, the dockside Brooklyn bar you never wanted. Your brother's being patient about it. He knows I can't work until I can work. Well, he just about has to be. When I called him, when I found you, he was in the middle of a piece.

Some poor girl has only one of Mick's lips tattooed on her ass because Mark broke down and couldn't finish. I think I hate this girl. That's a tattoo Timmy would've loved. A gnomic little paramecium, obscurely romantic. Among so very many regrets that Mark and I share, this one *smarts*. I am deeply covetous of this poor girl's fucked-up tattoo and Mark is deeply ashamed of it.

Not being able to work is about the worst sin Mark can think of. In the days following your heroic leap, he let one of his boys go into the ring without anyone at all in the corner. Kid's face got all smashed up, an event which turned Mark around, but good. Now he works all the time. If he's not running the bar, he's training some kid to be an amateur prizefighter. And if he's not doing that, he's learning how to tattoo something other than anchors and lips.

I don't think he ever sleeps, he works so hard. But Mark is

15

fair, if nothing else. So he's not about to suggest I start working again until I'm ready. Still, I think he knows what I'm up to.

For three weeks now, I've been opening up Mark's bar early in case you come in. It's a sucker's game, really, because you're dead. Besides, when you were alive you hated the bar and weren't often in town and when you were, you were sleeping with me, and when a man's sleeping with me, he's usually not up early and doesn't often dream, or so you used to say.

But I can't help it. Some bartenders will tell you that they can smell trouble the moment it pokes its briny-smelling head in the door. Most bartenders, Mark among them, say this. But they're bluffing, I think. They've got to be. I've been looking for trouble for three weeks now. End result? Nothing. Boredom. Booby trap.

Mark tells me you used to come in now and again to consult with Boris, the bouncer, your father's old bouncer, who sleeps most nights on the radiator in the ladies' room. Boris is a hopeless old rum-dumb, the term they used to use back when his drinking first became hopeless, and I tend to doubt he could actually bounce anyone if it came to that, but he had a prodigious, if that's the word, career as a dream analyst on the carny circuit some forty-five years ago. My God, Tim, for a showman yourself, right down to your balls, what a sucker you were for all that crap.

I unlock the bar just before dawn each morning and flick on the neon sign, which in that primary light by the old Red Hook wharves reflects first pink then green on the iced-over cobble sidewalk. Balustrade. What kind of name is that for a dead longshoreman's bar?

I fire up the crusty Irish Stew, the *stobhach*, as Mark calls it. Like your dad, he always keeps a pot abubble on a hotplate for his more unfortunately disposed customers. It's thick, covered with a dusty beige hat of old fat. The mutton and onion smell is horrifying. No one ever wants any and I'm starting to think it's the same stew your father kept. Not the recipe. I mean I think it's the *exact* same stew.

Then I close my eyes and sink against the counter and listen as you grunt opening the door.

"That ol' Chinaman up yet," you'd say, or something like it.

"He's a Gypsy," I'll say, but you'll be gone.

I set to cleaning the taps and a minute or two later you guys are back at the bar, Boris asking for whiskey, by which he means *gorzałka*, and you for whiskey, by which you mean absinthe. I used to ask for whiskey too, by which I meant *Bacanora Real*.

We're all fools, trapped in our little romances. I suppose it pleased us once to imagine that Mark has a midget beat cop stashed under the olives who'd pop out and haul us down to the Brooklyn House of D. for drinking mildly illegal imported rotgut. In fact, the new beat cop does come in every once in a while. He orders tomato juice, by which he means whiskey.

Of course, everyone who comes into a bar, this bar anyway, is slinging his own story, one way or another. I kind of like it. It's just that I loved you, Timmy and I love Mark, and even old Boris, sort of, and that makes me want to think of us as something special.

Your dreams were ludicrous, anyway, Tim; full of light and grace and comedy, signed Louisville sluggers as penises, petalled goddamned tulips as cunts, and most of the time, if I recall, you got to fly. Well, that joke was on you, anyway. It turned out you couldn't. Not really.

I haul a keg of weak Harp Lager up the stairs. I picture you, huddled with Boris, discussing a dream of your usual ilk and I can't understand why it disturbs you as it did. I can't understand why you're such a blessed motherfucker. That joke's on me, I guess.

Why are you huddled there with Boris, settled into a scarred banquette for the great interpretation of the dark, life-altering dream? Why don't you come to me? Okay, don't answer. I don't expect you to answer. I was using a blunderbuss technique there. I realize that. It's just—It's just that my sharpshooting's a little rusty, Tim.

Let me try again. What is the nature of your baffling dream? I know. You're working a children's science museum in Philly, though you've never actually been in Philly. You're hungry so you decide to take a break. You storm out of the sound check, as was your wont, and step out on the Champs Elysées to wolf down a cheese steak. As you eat, a dollop of melted cheese falls to the sidewalk and scuttles away like a mouse.

Something like that, right? I shouldn't laugh, although this is supposedly the dream of a wormwood junkie. Shouldn't laugh since I made this dream up. Shouldn't laugh because maybe if I'd been a better dream interpreter, or Mark had, or Boris had, we would've seen some threat in those beautiful dreams. Maybe, but I doubt it.

I dust the call bottles and line them up like happy little soldiers. I shouldn't laugh. Sick memories of my own, one or two beer-inspired, night terrors fill my mouth. Instead of laughing, I swallow to flood my throat with those sore, hacked-up half-images, blocking the guffaw as it forms. Instead of laughing I bring you each an empty shot glass, in time to hear you, Timmy, all awe and gentle charisma, ask what it means, in time to see Boris take my lover's hand and say

"You will be betrayed, but you won't mind."

God knows what I mean by that. Mark seems to think this is better for me than sitting around obsessing about the cat. I trust him, so I am keeping busy. Busy opening The Balustrade just before dawn. Busy sitting by myself in the pink and green bar light. Busy aching in each place your body broke. Busy waiting for the bogeyman.

I'm mad at Boris, anyway. I asked him to read my cards and he said, "classy, Iz. Tease the washed-up drunk. Why not just set me on fire one night and be done with it?"

And when I pressed, he spat. And said "You don't need the tarot, Kid. Every fact is available to you, except the one you need."

I can't be bothered to set the drunken old gypsy on fire, it's true. But still, I'd prefer it if he didn't out and out curse me with all that damned *Bohunk* gravitas.

Of late Mark's been bugging me about how I actually met you, Timmy. I guess I don't want to discuss it with him. I open my mouth, then close it, or gag it with a cigarette. Mark's sad in his old wooden bar, and wants to make some awful, breathtaking mythology of your life.

I think I want no part of it. I think I can't stand my part in it. Where are those cigarettes? I think I don't have the answer to his questions.

How did I actually meet you, Tim? It's a puzzle best resolved by spitting it out, probably, by offering the curiosity seekers and journeymen, the gawkers, firsts-of-May, drunken rabbis, stentorian con men, and even Mark, the single stern admonition: okay. Here it is. Happy Trails. Pack a gas mask.

But I'm not wont to resolve things at all, let alone in the best way. See, I like to tell Mark the truth whenever possible, but the truth about how I met you, Tim Acree, isn't something your brother could easily comprehend. Certainly I don't understand it. I never strove to. I really didn't.

My mother, drawn on her deathbed, was still struggling with what she viewed as the pointlessness of it. She was more than willing, I think, to buy into any crazy shit I offered by way of explanation. But I had no explanation at all. What could I say?

It all started with a cat? It has its roots in a kind of punk rock absurdity? It has its roots in a whacked-out allegory of yearning? It's all bound up with the history of a tenement airshaft?

In the end, her end, I was still opting for nothing. For a shrug, punctuated by the occasional deadpan declarative "what." As her last act, bemused as ever, she sent you from her bedside, and crooked me in with fingers both bony and swollen. I don't particularly believe in great swaths of chick wisdom, transmitted through the ages, but I was breathless anyway. When I leaned in, she said, only,

"Are those boys circumcised?"

"What boys? You mean Tim and Mark? The Acree boys?"

She nodded as I said "yes," then nodded again. And then she died.

I didn't think about that conversation for years, and then when I did, I couldn't tell whether she'd been asking, simply, had I seen their penises, or, the rather more complicated: is there anything redemptive at all about what my crazy daughter's doing with her life? Or, perhaps more poignantly, who are those clowns?

Who are those clowns? To Mark I am, for now, anyway, apprenticed as a bartender, and voluntarily, gratefully enslaved. And Tim? What are you? What were you? Neither angel nor husband, certainly; not companion nor Mephistopheles, nor even that tongue-sweet lie, *friend*. No, partner in crime is probably closest.

And what was the nature of our malfeasance? A damn good question, although not one easily asked or answered with dear Mark as the sounding board. I will say it here, and only once. On, what, December 20th (there's that punk declarative again—in truth, I know that date as I know the soft crease of each of your cocks in repose) now ten years ago, in an old tenement airshaft in a very big city, Tim Acree and I, Izzy Oytsershifl, did willingly forge a yearning so ravenous that, almost at once, it was clear that its fulfillment would kill us.

So far, it's only got you.

Me? I'm working in Mark's bar. I'll be here while I'll be here, polishing your urn, and ignoring it. I'll be here 'til I burst that boil. While I tend to your cat and your fucking fleas. For the foreseeable future. Unless I take off for Bogota. I'll be here while I'll be here. Until I blow. Boo.

3. CUSTOMER

Cam ◆ Carbon ◆ Cardboard box ◆ Casket-sized ◆ Checkerboard ◆ Clipper ◆ Combustion Correlation ◆ Cosmo ◆ Cover-up ◆ Crack ◆ Crank ◆ Cremation ◆ Creeps ◆ Cried ◆ Customer

C is for Customer. I am starting to miss my own work, Tim. Or rather, Mark's early morning customers are starting to give me the creeps. Not that it makes much difference how I say it. I don't miss my work because I don't feel anything and I don't have the creeps because I don't feel anything.

Feelings are for those whom chance has not written off. I am a machine. A fabulous machine with depression cylinders and mourning cams and cranks too cranky to think much of anything about other people's awe or joy or even obsession. I am not a very good bartender.

I am a machine except at my center. I'm a broken-hearted, broken-spirited homunculus trapped in a beer-burning heat engine that keeps making wry jokes and putting one damn foot in front of the other so no one can tell.

Nevertheless, the denizens of The Balustrade are starting to get on my nerves. Mark's not making it any easier. He's taken to using all your father's old bar slang and I can hardly understand him. I am, he says, "fighting the mirror," which is what painfully hungover people do, slumped sullenly at the bar, making walls of their forearms, before they've had enough to forget that they're hungover.

Apparently, it's a dangerous business, this fighting the mirror.

Not that I care. But Mark is worried about it and has extracted from me the promise that I will come up with some plan not to commit suicide for at least a few months. This I have agreed to in exchange for his not scattering your ashes in The Balustrade.

I have not agreed not to kill myself. I have only agreed to come up with a plan not to. Just as he did not agree not to have your long body torched, and did not agree not to keep the urn in The Balustrade. He has only agreed not to dump the results all over the fucking bar. This way, by inches, do we convince everyone that we're healing.

C is for Cremation, Tim, which I guess is some kind of tradition in your family. If you weren't so dead, safe from the blades of my guilt, I'd wanna be on record as having been vociferously against it.

"Tim loved bugs," I said.

"So?"

"So, shouldn't we return him to them? Let him nourish the dirt from whence they crawl and all that?"

"Acrees favor cremation."

"Tim loved bugs."

"Acrees favor cremation."

"Do Acrees favor leaping out of fucking windows, too?"

"Let the boy rest in peace, Izzy."

"Let the boy get e't, Mark."

Let's close the curtain on the rest of that conversation. It got ugly, Timmy. It ended in violence. And then violent sex. And then silence, and horror. And then silent sex. And you going up in flames. But I'd sooner walk this earth the rest of my allotted days then let him cast your remains in The goddamn Balustrade.

Coogan, like me, is fighting the mirror. He comes into the bar every morning and slumps there. His nose is an awful red potato, and, on his temples, the snake is out. The snake is out;

that's Irish barkeep slang too. I mean to say an angry blue vein pulses from his eyebrow to his ear. Framed by thin white hair, yellow 'cause he never washes it. Framed by yellow hair turned white with age then yellow again with dirt.

Coogan is like me, in that we are both fighting the mirror. He is also like you. He worked on ships 'til he had enough money to go become a forensic anthropologist. Like both of us, me because I appear to be in a state of intractable grief, and you because you are dead and were too busy reviving the Flea Circus to do much in the professorial line when you were alive, Coogan does not work in his chosen field anymore. I can only assume that he drank himself out of a job. I do not know what's brought him back to The Balustrade after all these years.

He drinks shot after shot of whiskey quietly and his blue eyes, like my horse-brown ones, are growing empty. Some late mornings we do not either of us have to fight the mirror because we can look across the bar at each other and watch the sparks die.

Coogan desperately wants a cover-up job on his ancient anchor tattoo and Mark won't give it to him. Mark won't tattoo a drunken man and Coogan is never sober. Sooner or later, he bugs me about it every day and I'm not sure what to say.

Mark and I are drifting further and further apart as he embraces morality and I falter. But in matters of ink I can only bow to his superior expertise. I cannot deny that once upon a time, armed with much Bacanora, a threaded needle and a crusty bottle of India ink, I did give you a crude jailhouse tattoo, Tim. But Mark is an expert of sorts, at least when it comes to anchors and Mick Jagger's lips. Questioning his pronouncements seems impossible to me.

Though, in truth, I never saw the harm in obliterating the blurry old anchor, turning it into a pair of Mick's lips even, if that's what Coogan wanted. Though, in truth, a cruel notion with regard to Coogan's tattoo has seized hold of me.

One morning this week, so early it was also the night before, Coogan was at the door as I made my way down cobbled Conover Street. The wind off the water ripped litter around in little funnels at his feet.

"Morning, Coo."

"I've been here since the age of Pericles."

"Banging at the door?"

"Banging to wake the damned which I guess means Boris isn't."

"Boris isn't. Damned, I mean, or here."

"No?"

"He went to a family reunion in the Catskills."

"Little girl, never lie to a thirsty old man."

"He's probably asleep. C'mon in. You can have some *stobhach*."

"Izzy, I didn't eat that godawful stew the day Leland Acree dragged the sheep's corpse in here and butchered it. You could smell it clear across the Buttermilk Channel. You think I'm gonna eat it now?"

"Well, how 'bout a drink then, Coo," I said, rolling up the gates and he smiled, weakly, then fell silent.

An hour passed. Or maybe two. Boris stumbled out of the ladies' room, clapping Coogan on the shoulder as he aimed himself at the door. A young man in a park's department uniform arrived across the street and sauntered aboard the old clipper which has turned into a waterfront museum. Boris returned with a day-old Portuguese roll, skimmed some of the fat off the *stobhach* with a plastic butter knife, plopped it on the roll and stumbled back into the ladies' room.

He waits 'til full sun-up before starting to drink. I cleaned the bar and waited. I waited for you. Coogan waited until he'd had enough to drink. I lined the shots up for him, waiting.

"Why don't you do it for me, Izzy?"

"You ever see one of my tattoos, Coo?"

"Can't say as I have."

"Mark has. Trust me, I don't have the touch. Ask Mark."

"Mark," he said, and laughed. "Mark the shark."

An hour passed. Or two. Boris came out, grabbed a bottle, stumbled into the ladies' room. Two old-fashioned made guys, a pair of venerable *goombahs* came in, ordered cognacs, lit cigars, sat in a corner, reviewing their past triumphs. Eighty-year-old men, nostalgic for the time Joey Chickens left Baby John's Sinatra LPs on the roof of his GTX.

The beat cop came in, cast a glance at the senile *mafiosi*, rolled his eyes. I served up his tomato juice. He peered at me and hitched up his belt, shyly. The little mace canister banged against the bar. He is young and slim. His utility belt rides too low on his hips.

"My wife thinks you need to start dating, Izzy."

Coogan looked up, his wrinkled old face twinkling with false amusement.

"Your wife is a modern woman, Officer," he said. "She's been to college. She reads *Cosmo*. She teaches adult literacy in Bed Stuy."

"I guess that's right."

"Leave Izzy be. She ain't so sophisticated. Her heart's in the grave."

"How 'bout it?" the cop said, turning to me.

"Freshen that juice for you?"

"No. Thanks. I'll be pressing on. If you change your mind, my wife's starting a grief support group in that Basque social club. Out in Greenpoint?"

"Okay. Thanks. I'll let you know."

He moved out the door. Coogan chuckled.

"You're a sour old jackass, you know that, Coo?"

"Yep."

"What do you want to turn that anchor into, anyway?"

He rolled his shirtsleeve, revealing the cruddy old piece, the ink green-black and spread. An anchor tattoo, more than half a century old, the size, shape and color of the Gowanus Canal.

"I've been giving that a whole lot of thought."

"And?"

"And I think I want to turn it into a fish."

"A fish? Jesus, Coo. An anchor practically is a fish."

That stopped him.

And a conspiracy formed whole in my mind. Like it was always there, and I, just then, ran into it.

"Will you do it for me, Izzy? I will pay richly."

"I don't need your money, Coo."

"We could do a trade."

"A trade," I said emptily.

Empty comes easy to me. In fact, I had willed him to say it. Mark will be mad, I thought, but glad too when he thinks about it. At least I have enough life force left in me to impose my will on a broken-down old man.

"A trade," I said. "A trade like what?"

"I only got three things I do, so it'll have to be one of them."

I wiped a wet ring from the bar in front of him. It left a stain which immediately sought camouflage in the Möbius strip of old water stains on the ancient oak slab between us.

"I can drink. I can identify remains. And I can make my wife cry. Any of those interest you?"

"When you say 'identify remains,' does that include—"

"*Cre*mains? Ah, now. That was my specialty. Lawyers used to line up for me, fork money over to make sure it was really Old Aunt Hattie in that urn. Twice a year the government would drag me out to Hawaii to identify shipments of burnt-up so-called MIAs. That's a hoot, let me tell you. Toward the end, I had to airlift in a case of bourbon. And the big joke was, pieces were most always pieces of Charlie anyway. But, Izzy?"

He peered at me.

"You're not stupid enough to think it ain't really Tim in there?"

"No," I said, "but there's these pieces."

"Pieces," he snorted. "That's a word I'm heartily sick of. Pieces. A body comes out of the retort with whole pieces intact. The pelvis just cracks open, usually. The fucking Loins of Man. 1700 degrees and it just twists a little. And what do we do with it? Mate? Gyrate on a dance floor? Hula-Hoop?"

He spit and sighed.

"Coo?"

"The cremains are swept out and ground under a magnet. Even then there are pieces. There are always pieces. My wife thinks I threw it all away 'cause of the gruesome nature of the work. But I liked the work, sifting through ashes and all, the pieces."

"Well, that's how you do it, right? The pieces? The not-powder pieces?"

"So?"

"So, I wouldn't mind knowing what part of Tim the pieces were."

He drank grimly. One shot. Two. Four. He sat fighting not the mirror, but the interlocking rings on the bar; not his countenance, but his own basest impulses. The snake pulsed and slithered on his temple.

"It's a bad idea," he said finally. "It'll hurt us both."

"It'll hurt the pain," I said.

"Alright. If you're sure."

"I'm sure, but what do you need?"

"Need? Nothing. A microscope. A light-box. A grid. I got it all at home. What do *you* need?"

"Need? Nothing. A needle. Some thread, ink. Alcohol, I guess, I mean as a disinfectant."

"I got that too."

And so I put Boris behind the bar and we grabbed two bottles and had us a little adventure. I was so excited I almost left without you, grabbing your urn only at the last second. In his well-lit South Brooklyn basement, Coogan gave me the short course on cremation.

Cremation is a tradition in your family, Tim. And now I'm the family expert.

You were burned in a casket-sized cardboard box. Your bones turned black as the carbon took over. The combustion destroyed all your organic compounds and once that was done, your bones turned white again.

You were a tall man, Tim, and a lean man, but there isn't a whole hell of a lot of correlation between your body's weight and the volume of your ashes. Most adults produce between 2.2 and 8.8. pounds of ashes. Yours weighed 3.6. And the lean doesn't count for much in the retort. Except that Coo says you probably burned slowly because there wasn't much fat to fuel the fire.

There are eight fragments from your shinbones, Timmy. Coogan can tell because the tibia splinters into a checkerboard pattern as it chars. The surface of a femur cracks into crescent moons and there is one piece from your lovely thighs. The ossicle from one of your ears is intact, although the heat of the oven has shrunk it to the size of a doll's ossicle.

There are two surgical clips among your mortal remains,

one of tantalum and one of stainless steel. Coo thinks there must have been more, that maybe they got lost when the cremation attendant swept your ashes out of the oven. I like these especially because they once tied your blood vessels safe. There is also about a fifth of a porcelain tooth which I didn't know you had.

I like having them, knowing which piece is which. I put different pieces deep inside me and carry them around all day like *Ben Wa* balls. In the morning I wonder: what shall I take with me today? Your femur? Your tibia? The little titanium post from your secret porcelain tooth?

Mostly it's your shinbone, but that is a statistical decision, I guess, and not a symbolic one. Most of the pieces, after all, are from your shinbones. Still, I suppose some symbolism is involved. I loved your long shins as they swung from your windowsill, and when I draw them out at night, I am giving birth to that section of you which turned me on most.

I am drawing you forth, Tim. I fetishize the pieces of your mortal remains, in chips and cracks, in chips from my crack, and that makes me a kind of miracle worker. Nothing fancy, you understand. I'm a worker of a minor, pedestrian sort of miracle. You're five weeks dead, and I am fucking you still.

The anchor came out pretty good, by the way. I turned it, best I could, into an ugly old grouper which made even Coo smile. Of course, Mark was furious at me; he always is nowadays. It's only a matter of time before he starts blaming me for your death. But when I gave him the tantalum surgical clip, he cried.

4. Delayed Menstruation

Darlin' ◆ Dangerous ◆ Dead Lover ◆ Deep Waters ◆ Delayed Menstruation ◆ Deliberate Depression ◆ Design ◆ Developed ◆ Dissolution ◆ Distaff ◆ Done ◆ Drogheda ◆ Dying Words

D is for Delayed menstruation. D is also for depression. Either can cause the other and I am, I'm sorry to say, prey to them both. I am in deep waters now. I am in deep waters now, even I can see that, but my mind is still sharp. It has not escaped my understanding, for example, that a baby could lie at the root of both depression and delayed menstruation.

I am not an artist like my dead lover. I'm a rationalist, a creature of science like my dead lover was before he became an artist. Well, I guess if a man becomes an artist, he always was one once. I should rather say that I am becoming exclusively what my dead lover was only in part, a creature of science.

I suppose since I am such a creature, or am becoming one, I should probably get a pregnancy test, but I have applied a deliberate logic to the mess of my motivations, as a creature of science always must, sooner or later, and I have determined that my desires are indeterminate. I would not like to be pregnant and I would not like to not be pregnant. Either option is undesirable.

The three possibilities and their Pythagorean inter-relationships imprison me. It is all I can do to maintain a decent sense of humor. It is all I can do to push on them a little with my tin cup, bending the bars, so that I find myself by turns, now trapped in an isosceles triangle, now a scalene. But most often I am unable to affect the possibilities, and my jail becomes equilateral, ghastly in the same measure on every side.

I am pregnant and therefore depressed because my lover is dead and also therefore not menstruating because the child within me has need of my latest efforts in the uterine lining department. Or else I am not pregnant, but depressed, and am therefore not menstruating, because my lover is dead. Or I am depressed because my lover is dead. Or because I am not pregnant, and am therefore alone and always will be, because not only is my lover dead, but he has left me without a baby to remember him by.

Or else I am suffering from both delayed menstruation and depression because I am pregnant, but not with my dead lover's child.

In the roof-top apartment, two floors above The Balustrade, the apartment you were a baby yourself once in, Tim, I sat cross-legged at your brother's feet, sipping at an awful mug of sweet Irish tea, huddled in my stupid triangle, not telling him. Why would I tell him? What good would it do?

Mark is tall like you but dark and strong; his rib cage, expanding shallowly in and out, blocked my view of everything else. He is gentle with me, because he loved you, Timmy, and because morality of a certain sort has become a comfort to him, but he is a dangerous man, brooding and huge, with eyes like a desert and great pink hands. I do not think he much likes me anymore.

For most of his life he was an amateur prizefighter and he looks like it. His face is flatter than it should be, and lumpy with scar tissue. He has a reputation as the best corner-man, or second, in Brooklyn. He is, they say, a genius with carpenter's wax and adrenalin chloride, and can keep a willing boxer going for hours after any sane ref would have sent him home.

He is, in short, the big heap quick-fix master of all wounds, large and small. It is no surprise to anyone that he cannot heal himself, that your death has, as they say, floored him. That was somehow to be expected. But it is a matter of great puzzlement to him, and to all those he represents, that he has not found a way to fix me. He is, as I've said, starting to hate me for it.

When he finished his tea, he hurled the mug against the wall and asked me if I had come up with a plan yet. The steadfast mug, no doubt smuggled into this country up your great-grandmother's Drogheda ass, broke into two, easily glueable halves. My God, how terrible that sounds. I don't mean it like that, Timmy. It's just that your damn brother is getting so fucking *Irish* as he mourns. It's just that I hadn't yet come up with a plan.

Frankly, until that moment, I hadn't even bothered to try. It is apparent to me, even though I don't speak here with the authority of an expert, even though I don't have the habit of them cuts, as the prizefighters say about Mark, that there will be no quick fix for me.

It is apparent to me that, publicly, at least, I am losing my shit in the most irritating possible way to a great corner-man. I am becoming reasonable. So that the weaker I get, the more vital I seem.

With reason in my corner, I'm sure I probably could have come up with a suitable plan to prevent my own suicide, one that would conform to all the rigorous demands of that other sweet science, reason. But when I tried to puzzle it out, it occurred to me that if I can continue to appear to become rational, I will eventually appear so rational that I will cease to be human, and at that point, I will, in effect, have killed myself anyway.

But I am young, and not all that rational yet, my nasty talk notwithstanding, and lonely in my triangle, and when he asked me, so earnest and sad and drunk, I could not resist the urge to draw him into the ring with me.

This is not something a boxer conventionally does with his second, nor a widow with her mate's brother. It is not done because it implies that one's fight is not really one's own. It is not done because it is, in some way, cruel to both parties involved.

"Yeah," I said. "For the moment my plan is to stay alive until I get my period."

"What does that mean?"

"You know what it means, Mark. A woman sheds her uterine lining, once a month or so, with the moon some say—"

"Unless."

"Yes. Unless."

He took my mug from me, filled it at the kitchen counter, then handed it back solicitously. More Irish tea, black and sweet and strong, bought by the pound from a man driving a dray. Or something.

Mark leaned into the hassock that had sat with me at his feet moments before. His legs, long like yours but thick, spread out to embrace me. He gestured, can I have a sip, and took back the mug he'd just handed me. He drained most of it. Then he hurled my mug against the wall too.

"A baby?" he choked. "Timmy's baby?"

"Timmy's baby," I said. "Or yours."

He is sentimental. And growing more Irish, more like I guess your father was, by the day. I shouldn't mock. It seems to be working for him.

But he stood and roared. He knelt and wept. He began to riff on the miraculous gift it all was, and something distaff rebelled in me.

"What am I supposed to do with a baby, Mark? Feed Timmy's fleas on it?"

"Izzy."

"That would be good, actually. He fed some of the fleas on

his arm. Ulysses, Priam, Laöcoon — all the fleas in the finale. They say human-fed fleas are strong."

"Izzy."

"What?"

"Get out."

"Are you casting me out, Mark?"

"Izzy."

"What?"

"Please get out."

Who am I kidding? I'm caught in your wake, Timmy; headed straight for damnation. So, of course I'm not pregnant. How could I be pregnant? There'd be some redemption in that.

I'm just looking for something, anything to hold onto. A carton of Chinese food would do.

Even Mark knows nothing so neatly beautiful is going come from all this. Pregnant? With you dead, and both of us lost? My God, it would argue for Design.

Who are we both kidding? Mark called me at our house late the same night, his voice hoarse.

"Izzy? Do you have a plan B?"

"Hey, Mark. I'm glad you called. I'm so sorry about—"

"Izzy?"

"I'm studying the angles, Mark."

He sighed.

"Tell me what he said again."

"He said: 'I'll stop by the knackers on the way home.'"

"Sure and that meant what you say?"

Now I sighed.

"I took him to mean we were too broke to eat take-out but he'd get some anyway because he knew neither of us would feel like cooking. Knackers. Horse meat. Get it? Jesus, Mark. How many times do we have to go over it?"

Silence and I've blown it again. I sit and breathe into the red telephone we bought in San Francisco, listening to your brother do the same. I sit and rip the hairs out of my leg one by one. I wish I could give myself over to this boy's sweet blandishments, Timmy. Honest to God, I do. Just let myself get soothed. But I can't.

I would if I could. But I can't.

So I don't.

"Did he get the take-out, then?" the phone said into my ear, after a time.

"No."

His voice broke and he hung up, calling back before I could even find a cigarette.

"It's not enough," he said.

"Tell me about it."

"Should you be telling people something else then, do you think?"

"Like what?"

"That would be for yourself to know. Wouldn't it then?"

"For fuck's sake, Mark. Would you stop talking like that?"

"Sorry."

"No. Listen, *I'm* sorry. But what do you want me to say? He didn't leave a note. I wasn't there. I didn't hear his exit lines. What should I do? Hold a séance?"

He was quiet.

"Just make them up, Izzy," he said finally.

"Make them up? I don't know what the fuck he was thinking. What if I'm wrong?"

"If you're wrong, you're wrong. I'm sure Tim won't mind. He's dead. G'night, Darlin'."

He really is the sweetest boy alive, your brother. I'm not so absorbed in my rapid dissolution that I can't see how hard he's trying. And, well, I could do that, I guess, Timmy. Make up your dying words. I'll study on it. But it's not going to keep me alive for very long.

I'm not going to get it right. I'm not an artist and I don't stand in a state of grace. I'm just me, plodding along. One paw in front of the other. There can't be a glorious transformative moment because I'm just a creature of science, which makes me want to review the facts.

Facts of you, Timmy. Facts carved into a mountain of feeling and memory. Shifting facts. These don't yield too well to deliberate logic, which is the only tool I have at the moment.

I am trying to remember.

Who were you, Timmy? Almost six weeks ago when you were alive, who were you? At times all I can think is: you were dumb. Dumb to jump when I loved you so much I'd have taken a bullet for you. And that must have some objective value. I can't correlate the value, true, but maybe that's because *I'm* dumb.

I'm dumb. I'm the big dummy, not you. Because while it's true that I would've taken a bullet for you. True that I loved you that much. And probably true that, all by themselves, those facts have some objective value. There's an aspect to this equation that I keep overlooking.

I already *took* the bullet. *You're* the fucking bullet. Dying words possibility #17: "Sure and *Ich bin gezen* the fucking bullet." Dying words possibility #578: "Man oh man, is Man Ray cool." Dying words possibility #4280: "Geronimo."

5. SAINT EVLALIA.

Ease ◆ Eerily ◆ Embarrassing ◆ Epilogue ◆ Equipped ◆ Eschaton
Eternity ◆ Eulogy ◆ St. Evlalia ◆ Evoking ◆ Excruciating ◆ Exegesis ◆ Exit Line

E is for St. Evlalia. Over our bed hangs a picture of a girl. She is not pretty, but her dark eyes burn with an intensity that makes a certain kind of person look twice. Her skin is a lightish olive. Her hair the impossible color of a fine single malt. Her tattered bedclothes and the misty room around her are an artist's conception of medieval. Her face is flat and oval; the bones of her eye sockets, prominent, heightened by the purple gullies under them, so incongruous on that young face that they look, in the picture, like racing stripes painted on a car.

The picture looks enough like me as a teenager that my own mother, after peering at it, declared "so *by you* this a life, posing for the goyim?"

(*"Izzy," she would say, she would always say, "these are not your people."*)

Anyhow, the picture isn't me. The picture was printed in the shop of one Maxwell Arnisch, Ivar Place, London. In 1947. Years before I was born. You bought it at Portobello Road, that stronghold of used C. of E. crap, years before you met me.

The picture is a saint card from some long-gone Catholic schoolgirl's collection. St. Evlalia. Who died at age twelve. Who spent her nights catching the fleas in her blanket, separating them by sex, then letting them go.

None of the saint books, not even the good ones, seem to know whether, "*by her,*" this was a kind of prayer. Or just an act of simple self-flagellation. But you preferred to think it was a kind of prayer.

The exegesis of a flea's body was a kind of prayer for you too, Timmy. Hot summer nights, running your fingers over my naked back, you'd absently trace a flea along my spine. I knew it was a flea and not some secret message of love because I could feel your forefinger changing pressure as it moved from head to thorax to abdomen. Ten segments of abdomen. Three segments of thorax. Six legs.

One head. You always saved the head for last.

If I woke crying from a nightmare and crawled across the crack in our horrible trundle bed, you'd hold my hips and repeat the same words in an endless soothing loop.

"Order *siphonaptera* in the endopterygote section of the neopterous division of the pterygote subclass of the class insecta," you'd say. Over and over, as if to say: all's right with the world.

I mean to say that seeing St. Evlalia's mania as prayer wasn't much of a leap for your imagination. I mean to say I may have, eerily enough, looked liked her, but it was obviously you who had her soul.

Although, come to think of it, I doubt if little St. Evlalia ever wanted to *be* a flea. It was freaky for me, Timmy, the night we first had sex, how you'd use your feet as well as your hands to caress me. Not that I had some weird Eastern horror of feet. Or that I hadn't, as they say, "done everything," by then. Just I wasn't used to thinking of feet as organs of touch.

I wrinkled my nose and you asked "s'up, Kid?" and I remember I struggled for a word. "No, don't stop," I said. "It's just, it seems . . ."

"Erotic?" you asked, so hopefully, grinning, I had to laugh.

"No," I said. "Sybaritic."

"Two pairs of palps, Kid. The better to read your skin."

And damned if you couldn't, Tim. Damned if those hands and feet and flashing eyes of yours didn't seem to register every nuance, every shudder, every change in pressure and temperature. A strange fact about us, Timmy. It stands alone in a little box at the back of my head. That the sex was so good, it was excruciating.

One night early on, I hid my face in my hands and wept. So raw and wrung out and overwhelmed, I was embarrassed to look at you. What you felt, I can't say, but what you did was jolly me out of it.

"You think that was good, Kid? C'mon, let's watch Ulysses."

You pulled me off the bed, over to the flea tanks. A journey of about a foot. A journey of a thousand years. No journey at all.

"I thought all those big ones were Ulysses," I said. "One dies, you train another."

"They are. All North American Giants. All male. All just under eight millimeters long. And all Ulysses. A thoroughly expendable commodity."

"So?"

"So, look," you said, unceremoniously plucking one Ulysses out of his tank, slapping your special magnifying goggles over my eyes. I looked first at myself, in the smoked glass of the Ulysses tank, and started. Beyond allowing for the close-up study of insects, your magnifying goggles had the additional feature of making the wearer *look* like an insect.

"They may be expendable," you said, "but each one is equipped with two penis rods, wrapped around each other."

"Like a caduceus," I said staring with no small awe at the black thing squirming in my lover's palm.

"Or a very ingenious dildo," you said.

"The 'Red Hook Wife-Tamer?'"

"Hey," you said, "even a Brooklyn boy can dream."

We tried it a couple of times, twisting one of my pink flexible curlers around your cock, but we never really got into it. The spongy extra width did nothing special for me, and you of course, couldn't feel it, having no nerves in my curlers.

But your point was your point. That the lowliest creature on God's green earth could have great sex. That the beatific was all around us. That "any flea, as it is in God is nobler than the highest of angels in himself." This from Meister Eckhart, who, since we're keeping track, E is also for.

And my point? My point is that you were so confident, Timmy. You moved through the world with absolute ease. That there should be a saint whose kind of prayer was identical to your own, that your lover looked just like the saint in question, that the sex you had with that lover suggested the Eschaton, all these you took as your right and due.

Neither coincidence nor bugs nor God's good grace scared you, Timmy. Why, then, I have to ask . . . no, wait. I think I don't have to ask that yet.

Unique among flea-related saints, which, curiously, are manifold, St. Evlalia is not invoked *against* fleas. She is invoked to protect those poor souls who, for no apparent reason, are simply wasting away. It was this picture, and not my sparkling exhortations across the airshaft, which first drew you to me.

But my resemblance to the picture doesn't interest me anymore. That kind of awe and wonder are reserved for those of us who are *not* wasting away. What I wonder about St. Evlalia is what I wonder about everyone dead nowadays. When she finally wasted away, was there a eulogy?

E is for exit lines, which is what we call the final words a person says. And E is for eulogy which is what we call it when someone still on stage takes that task upon themselves. A eulogy has the profundity of careful thought. The absent person is neatly summed up. If well done, the eulogy will evoke the person who has exited in such a way as to almost bring him alive for a moment. The listeners are moved. They laugh. And cry.

An exit line, on the other hand, is profound only in its stark absurdity. I've been collecting exit lines lately, Timmy. Stonewall Jackson: Let us cross over the river and rest in the shade of the trees. James Thurber: God bless, Goddamn. Saint Philip of Neri, the patron of Rome, who lived 1200 years after wee Saint Evlalia and nevertheless didn't make it to the groovy Summer of 1595, was heard to utter, laughing: Last of all, we must die. And General Robert E. Lee said only: Strike the tents.

These have passed into history because they carry with them some sense of prescience, and that comforts us. The speaker has stared death down and still has the strength for a final remark. When we hear these words, we feel that life has somehow triumphed over death. It gives us hope. We laugh. And cry.

Then there are those people whose dying words, even in hindsight, do not seem to speak to the issue of exit. Consider as exhibit, well, E, my mother's "are those boys circumcised?"

The speaker has no idea she is mouthing her final utterance. The words in question are starkly comic. The human condition itself is brought alive for us in this moment. And if we ourselves are human, we are moved by the beautiful pointlessness of it all. We laugh. And cry.

But the thing is, Timmy, what all these summations seem to have in common is that they serve as epilogue. They promise to bring the dead back to life, if only for a moment. They promise extra innings, Timmy. And then they don't deliver.

Because the truth is that the truth ("I'll stop by the knackers on the way home") works just as well as possibility #1108: "Mommy I hear the train," which works just as well as possibility #14: "Oh look, a mouse." They all bring you alive for just a moment. Because they can do no other. Because exit lines are structured that way.

I can't seem to make up your dying words, Timmy. Because the truth is that I don't really want you brought alive for just a moment. I want you not to be dead.

I dreamed you were alive last night, Timmy. I dreamed there'd been a huge mistake and you were still alive. My heart danced in my chest I was so happy you were alive. In my dream you were alive and living with Johnny Thunders who was also alive.

You guys were alive and in love and moving to California as soon as you could get the money together. You needed a lot. A hundred bucks from each of your friends to rent a '71 Road Runner to get there.

I'm nodding, a '71 Road Runner, uh-huh. Hurst 4-speed, you said. I'm smiling. Of course, a 426 HEMI. Of course, you said. Sub-lime green, Johnny Thunders piped up, elbowing you. With a black vinyl roof.

You rolled your eyes, Timmy, but so fondly. And ever so briefly I wondered whether Johnny Thunders' chicken-skinny legs could pump the bear-trap clutch on a Hurst 4.

You said you and Johnny were going to squat this land in Atlantic Beach when you got there. Atlantic Beach, I said. Atlantic Beach, *California*. It's an old Victorian resort town, outside San Francisco, Johnny explained.

You're going to squat some land, I said. In *Atlantic* Beach. On the sunny California coast. That's how we'll do it if we're smart, Johnny said. But we need a hundred bucks from each of our friends, you said. 'Cause the land costs 8.9 million dollars.

46

Just a hundred bucks, I said. From each of your 89,000 closest friends.

And then everyone can come, Johnny said.

You looked good, Timmy. Happy.

Hugging Johnny Thunders.

So, let me get this straight, I said. You and Johnny Thunders are going to rent a late model Mopar so you can start a commune in sunny Atlantic Beach. On the California coast. You and Johnny Thunders are going to become, what's the term I want, muscle-hippies?

My God, I said, your fans will club you to death.

My God, the fans, you laughed, Timmy.

Well, I said, even assuming your San Francisco fans can rouse themselves from their torpor to club you to death, I guess that'd be a pretty cool way to go. And I laughed. And you laughed. And Johnny Thunders laughed.

I know this dream is taking me a long time to relate. But what the fuck, Timmy. You've got an eternity. It's not as if you're going anywhere.

The point is I was so happy you were alive. I didn't care that you'd left me for Johnny Thunders or that you guys were hitting me up with quite possibly the stupidest story I'd ever heard. You were alive, Timmy. And standing right next to me.

I was happy. Because you were alive. And my heart was dancing in my chest.

And that's the only feeling I have interest in evoking. Not a half-fond look at the human condition vis-à-vis your mortality. Not a bittersweet recollection which brings you alive for just a moment. Not any kind of higher truth the listeners can find succor in. Not any kind of truth at all.

A lie.

Alive.

Dying words possibility #135: Dear Izzy, I have left you for a man. I'm sorry to hurt you but we are very much in love. Maybe you've heard of him. His name is Johnny Thunders. We are moving to California to start a muscle car commune. I am starting a new life and wish you all the happiness that I have found.

Or else dying words possibility #2002:

I'm not dead.

Facade ◆ Faceless ◆ Fantasizing ◆ Fatuous ◆ Fault ◆ Finale ◆ Fine ◆ Flaw ◆ Flea Circus
Flew ◆ Forever ◆ Formulaic ◆ Foster Father ◆ Foul Play ◆ Free Fall ◆ French Foreign Legion

F is for Flea circus. Most people, when I told them my boyfriend had a travelling flea circus, wanted to know if it was for real. He doesn't really *train* the fleas, does he, they'd ask. I mean, are they *live* fleas, or does he just glue them into place or is it all showmanship, or what?

And, taking my cues from Tim, I'd answer "yes." Yes, he trains them. Yes, they're alive. Yes, he glues them in place. Yes, it's showmanship. Yes.

A flea circus, like most attractions born out of nineteenth century English sideshows, *is* mostly about showmanship. You see what the "signor" or "professor" wants you to see. Much sleight of hand is involved, and storytelling. And indirection. So, yes, of course, there is much cementing in place of dead fleas.

I always wondered why this facet of the art, precise and demanding, struck people as a cheat. I mean, if you think about how tiny a flea is, making a costume and props for it is no walk in the park. And if you multiply that feat by the hundreds of dead, glued, costumed fleas necessary to make a tableau with a recognizable story, a wedding say, or an orchestra, you're suddenly talking about thousands of hours of labor.

To dress up his fleas, Tim used a technique developed by an order of Mexican nuns whose *pulgas vestidas*, tricked out as peasants, ladies of the evening, barkeeps, day laborers, fruit hawkers and even Texas Rangers, and mounted under shards of magnifying glass, have long been sold to tourists to raise money for the church. In a safety deposit box in Carroll Gardens, Tim kept his parting gift from the Sisters: an ancient diorama of Jesus, crucified. The piece had been with the nuns for so many countless decades that no one in the cloister remembered who had made it, or why.

The little scene came equipped with a crown of thorns made from tiny threads of dried flower stamen. Barabus is recognizable, or Caiaphus, I guess, depending on your interpretation; a hedgehog flea just barely peering like Kilroy over the floor of the little scene. There are jeering Romans in spades, of course.

A minute Mary Magdalene's evident, kneeling with a bucket and rag at the base of the cross. Well, seeming to kneel. I expect the nuns merely sawed her off, as it were. Tim liked that figure best. He always maintained that the Mary Magdalene flea was a male. A small matter of some very gentle gender-bending, to be sure, but it amused him greatly.

I have no reason to doubt Tim's authority on this subject, but it seemed to me, the few times we went to the bank to see the diorama, that the tiny Mary Magdalene positively exuded femininity. She was naked to the belly, her middle legs draped in a makeshift burlap sarong. Her bosom—well, to be precise I guess I mean her lack of bosom, was concealed by the thick black plaits of hair, obviously human, glued to her head.

I've mentioned the jeering Romans, their bristly black segments overlapping like lobsters'. To me, these were sharply distinguishable from the Money Lenders, whose bellies were each distended with some now long-dead nun's blood.

"Well, you have to admit the Temple was bloated," Tim said when I complained. "Anyway, you should be pleased with *La*

Monja's biblical accuracy. You're lucky there even *are* Romans."

"The Romans look strong, though, Timmy, and smugly satisfied. Look at those Jews. Look at my people. Look at their faces. They're so shifty. And. And, and they look so counter-revolutionary."

He cackled. In the sealed steel viewing closet the bank employee had led us to, his deep laugh filled every crevice.

"They're fleas, Izzy. They're not your people, unless there's something you haven't told me."

(*"Izzy,"* she would say, she would always say, *"these are not your people."*)

"You know what I mean."

"I do," he said swooping up and pressing me against the cold wall, kissing my nose. "But fleas don't have expressions, Kid. That's just the genius of this particular *Vestida*.

So there's that, too. There are live fleas. There are dead fleas, artfully arranged. And there's the unidentifiable something the viewer brings to the performance.

I don't think anyone who ever *met* Tim, let alone attended one of his performances, could have missed the fact there was about him something of the vaudeville magician. He was both dramatic and sneaky, his personality huge. But you were never quite sure if he was putting you on, never quite sure if maybe there wasn't something special about him, a gift, a *touch*.

Anyhow, while he was certainly one of the great showmen, he was, first, last, and always a Doctor of Fleas. After a while, it began to rankle Tim that people kept looking for the seams of his show, kept pointing out the showmanship as if it were a flaw.

"They should be focusing on the fleas," he said.

And thus the finale was born. Ah, the Trojan Horse. A great crowd-pleaser. And easy, in some ways, because the Greek fleas needed no costumes. When they poured forth from the tiny wooden horse, thousands of them, they could even be seen by the outermost circle of people crowded around Timmy's table.

Timmy built the horse himself, spring-loading its side so that Sinon, the Greek traitor, played nightly by an *Hystrichopsylla talpae talpae*, an English mole and vole flea measuring close to a quarter inch, could open it all by himself.

Watching Timmy tether Sinon with a piece of wire the approximate thickness of a baby's fine down was a thing of beauty. Watching Timmy methodically fill his horse, one at a time, with more than a thousand fleas, could drive a girl to distraction.

But in the end, his maniacal focus paid off. All the genius of Timmy's performance, all his hard work and dedication to the cause—it all came together in his finale. Because when those fleas flew, jaws fell. Gasps of wonderment escaped the crowd. And Timmy, as he always did when really pleased, would smile gently in his top and tails, retreating from the crowd a little as if to give all the credit to the fleas.

F is for Finale.

You loved a big finish, Timmy. Which leads me to many questions, none of which I'm asking. F is for Finale, Timmy, which makes me want to cry.

But I won't.

Because F is also for Fall. Oh, and for Foul Play. Matters I guess I should address. Because, quite simply, people like you don't kill themselves, Timmy. Skulking little poets with dried-up cunts kill themselves. Rock stars and overachievers and people wracked by self-loathing kill themselves. Mothers of dead children kill themselves.

People like me kill themselves.

But you, Timmy? A lapsed Catholic who never made a false step? A man who lived every day as if it were his last—fully, I mean, of course; not broodingly—a man in perfect health, who worked hard at what he loved, who, literally, made elevating the meek into an art form?

Timmy, my love, people like you don't kill themselves. People like you enter the fucking priesthood.

I know what you'd say. I mean, if you were alive to say it. You'd say people like me don't kill themselves either. People like me enter the French Foreign Legion.

Because the tough forget. You'd say the tender remember and that's their job. To survive, to bear witness. But the tough forget. Which means . . . Which means . . .

Oh, Timmy, you jerk. You wouldn't say anything like that. I don't know what you'd say. I never knew what you'd say. I conjure you to comfort myself and I can't think what you'd say. Everything you ever did came out of left field for me. I loved you, Timmy, because I couldn't fathom your depths. So I conjure you, but I put my own words in your mouth. And then I get mad. Because you sound so predictable.

But to get back to foul play. In a case like yours, one is tempted to suspect foul play, right? Because why would a guy like you kill himself? And because *if* a guy like you had some unfathomable reason for killing himself, he'd for sure want the world to know it.

Because Golden Boys don't kill themselves.

And Hams leave notes.

Flew. Flung. Flap. Flail. Flee. Flea. I note here, I *must* note here, without malice, or irony, or even, I hope, emotion, the preponderance of fl- words which can describe your blond-boy flight.

Lately I've been wishing that, in the matter of your flight, your mysterious death, foul play was still a going concern. I've been fantasizing that not only is foul play suspected by the powers that be, but that I myself am the suspect in question.

Sometimes I even imagine that not only am I the suspect in question, but that I actually pushed you out. This is tedious stuff, I know. Fatuous. Formulaic. I won't even get into its bearing on the Stages of Grief or whatever.

I feel guilty, yes. I'd like to be taken away and put in a metal cage where I don't have to think, yes. Yes, yes.

But more than all that, I wish I'd killed you, Timmy.

I wish I had killed you, Timmy. Killed you first before you killed me. Because then your death would have some meaning. It would be part of my life, an act I committed.

Maybe just by accident. You were leaning out the window, I was behind you, watering the fleas. I tripped on the cat, and fell into you. And down you went. Or maybe I was mad and hurled Altamont (Airshaft, I mean) at you. You went deep to save the cat. And away you flew.

I wish I could claim responsibility and get away with it; cry out that it was all my fault and get hauled away forever, beaten up by cops, clucked at by judges, fisted by cell mates who stink of bleach. If I thought I could get away with it, I'd try. But for one awful flaw, that would be my plan. I'd plant evidence, even.

But in this facet of escape you totally fucked me, Timmy.

I can't make your death into an act I committed because little Fuz saw the whole thing. He saw you manhandle the window open. He saw you perch on the sill. He saw you stand, grinning. He saw you grab the sash bottom with your fingers. He saw you trampoline your body back and forth. He saw your long ligaments gain momentum. He saw you hurl yourself out. And he saw you smile, as you hurried yourself along.

These things he reported to me, to Mark, to the investigating officers. He was freshly showered as he spoke. Beads of water stood on his hair and I stared at them, breathing his little-kid smell, listening to the sensible questions of the cops on the scene.

Uncle Willy's cracked brown hand, a bus driver's hand, was on Fuz's shoulder. Uncle Willy's gently guiding posture, the way he collected righteousness to himself like stardust, made me want to puke. I avoided his sympathetic eyes, and his foster kid's serious ones, like the plague.

Kindness was—is—a plague to me. It is kindness, more than anything else, that makes me want to claim responsibility for your death. Not my own kindness, prompting me to be honest, you understand, but the wretched, humanizing kindness of others. I want to be well away from kindness—of any kind.

Because when I stood there in shock, listening to Fuz and the cops and Uncle Willy and Mark murmur back and forth, I wanted to scream as if to shatter the walls around us, to sob oceans, to faint, at least to ask someone how am I supposed to live now? But their awful soothing kindness, that gentle steady pressure emanating from all five of them, even Mark who you know was broken himself—their kindness kept me together, inside myself.

All by myself inside myself. Spartan and ordered and fine. Their kindness gave me a skin, which isn't necessarily what a fractured person needs. So that when the murmuring stopped, and I saw by their ten kind eyes that it was time for me to say something, I couldn't remember what I wanted to say; couldn't remember that if they ever stopped murmuring I'd planned to ask the cops, or the foster father, or the older bro, or the wise child —ask one of the authority figures before me—just how in the goddamn world I was supposed to go on.

And so I said what I could think of to say, said

"A Timmy in free fall accelerates at a rate of 32.2 feet per second per second."

Alone among all the people in the entire world, only you, Timmy could have taken that as I meant it, which is to say to be measured identically with "how in the goddamn world am I supposed to go on?" And alone in the entire world, only you, Timmy, would've responded in the manner I craved, which is to say by laughing.

But I gotta give Mark and the cops and Uncle Willy and even little Fuz credit. I mean they didn't call a social service agency or anything. They looked at each other, and then the cops and the neighbors split, still murmuring regrets, and then Mark poured me a stiff drink. It all sheds new light on the expression "killing me with kindness."

Kindness. As *if*. As if there were anything in the world I wanted less.

There is a place in this world where kindness, if it exists at all, has mutated into a kind of laissez-faire survival strategy; a place where a well-timed smile, plastered on knowingly, is highly prized rather than pitied; a place where personal problems are best left at the door.

There is a place in this world called the Correspondence Division of the Tenders and Exchange Department of the Interstate Bank of New York and New Jersey. And there a cubicle awaits my return. It has awaited my return for almost two months now.

To say the cubicle awaits my return is to invest the cubicle with a certain humanity it never had. The cubicle is gray and beige. There are no pictures on its facade, or identifying marks of any kind. It is the policy of the Interstate Bank of New York and New Jersey that such decorations distract its stalwart employees.

By "it," I mean here, of course, the bank. Although I suppose there's no harm in thinking that I was (am), in effect, the cubicle's employee rather than the bank's. Except that to say I am the cubicle's employee, on leave now two months, is to be, I'm afraid, ironic.

I still catch myself being ironic every now and again,

ironic, world-weary, glib. These are tics, I guess. The last shreds of humanity. Which isn't what you'd expect, right? I mean you'd expect the needy hungers of infancy to be the last to go, or the mighty heart.

But all that's left of me are the ignoble tropes. Pride and sarcasm. Leftovers from that time when . . . when . . . when . . .

Well, never mind. We been there already.

My job awaits me! My delicious faceless corporate job! The job you said was killing me inside, Timmy. But all that's academic. Now.

7. Gush

Gain ◆ Get Real ◆ Get Straight ◆ Ghastly ◆ Giving up the Ghost ◆ Gloom ◆ Glop
(Billy) Goat Gruff ◆ Gossip ◆ Grace ◆ Grievous ◆ Grinding ◆ Grit ◆ Guilt ◆ Gush

G is for Gush. Volcanic gush. Biblical gush. Which is how my period started this morning. Well, not so much a period as a hemorrhage. But the idea is the same. I dreamed of a bus crash, watching from a bridge, and awoke staring down at my red thighs like Billy Goat Gruff at the troll.

The situation before me had two ready explanations, which I considered calmly as clots of black red tissue pooled beneath my ass. Either I had been willing my period's absence, in which case my body was taking the position that it could no longer pretend to be pregnant, no longer hold out the slim hope that I still had something of Tim to cling to. Or else I actually *had* been pregnant, and my body was now taking the position that it was in no shape to come through on that harsh, shining promise.

My body, it seemed, was bent on taking a position.

I was dizzy as I rose, and it occurred to me in that in either case, I appeared to be losing a lot of blood very quickly, and would probably need medical attention. A mop-up job at the very least. A D&C almost certainly. A transfusion. I.V. fluids. Antibiotics. And so I sat back down. To consider my options. Calmly.

Best of all I liked the possibility that I might die here in a pool of blood and Timmy would find me and be heartbroken. I kept coming back to the image of his ashen face. So long and blond and earnest, his face. His face staring down at the dead dead me. In a pool of blood. His endless fingers bending, curling to touch the blood, taste it. Take it inside himself as if only that would make it real. That would show him, right?

But again and again I had to remind myself that this was just not a realistic option. The circuitry of my thought loop was complex. To override it, I had to get stern. Take myself in hand. Get real. I might die here in a pool of my own blood. But Timmy would never know.

And so slowly the idea of attracting some medical attention to my side began to gain steam in my head. I mean, if Timmy's not going to know I'm dead, not ever going to mourn me the way I mourn him, not ever going to awake each morning with a thrashing catfish in his lungs, not ever going to cry himself dry so his eyelids stick shut with salt and glop—if Timmy's not ever going to know I'm dead, why not live forever?

But I didn't move. I sat quietly, sucking my fingernails, not moving. Not reaching for the phone. The cat crouched away from me, mewling. Still, I didn't move. Didn't call out for help. Didn't reach for the phone.

Because why live forever just to spite Timmy if Timmy would never know?

In fat, nineteenth century novels, the stunned protagonist, paralyzed by indecision, or the dying hero clutching the seeping wounds of injustice, invariably narrates this moment with a line like "how long I sat there, I knew not."

"How long I sat there, I knew not," a state of affairs I find incomprehensible. For exactly thirty-eight minutes by the blinking blue-green clock on the DVD player, I sat there.

And then the phone rang. I did not think it was the song of angels, come to carry me home. It did not bring me back to myself, call me from a tunnel of light, remind me of all I had yet to do. It simply rang. And on a reflex, I answered it. Simply. Sleepily.

"Good morning. May I please speak to Dr. Acree?"

"I'm sorry, he's dead. Can I take a message?"

"I—I—I beg your pardon?"

"No. God. I beg *your* pardon. I'm so sorry I said that. But, um, Timmy really is dead. Is there something I can help you with?"

The voice on the phone was young, male, nervous. But there was a hint of grit to it. And in the click of its inhaled breath, I felt it rally.

"I'm so sorry to hear that, Mrs.—?"

"Izzy."

"Izzy. Right. Well, anyway, of course I'm sure Dr. Guetta had no idea or he'd never've had me call. When did it—did he—when did he—"

"I think 'pass' is the euphemism you're going for there."

The voice on the phone had the grace to laugh, albeit awkwardly. I shifted my weight and felt a ghastly squirt of blood.

"It's about two months now," I said, preemptively, to cover my rising guilt.

What if the poor boy who owned the voice on the phone somehow found out he was making inane small talk with me as I sat there, giving up the ghost? Wouldn't you hate someone forever if they did that to you? Wouldn't you curse them to hell and back? If they made you a major player in their grand demise without giving you the choice? Made you an accomplice to their most grievous sin?

And he'd probably find out. He'd asked for "Dr. Acree," which meant he was an academic. And how long could it take for gossip to get around in the higher Flea-science circles? What else were they going to talk about? Fleas feed, mate, die and occasionally transmit disease. I mean, true he hadn't known Timmy was dead, but maybe he'd been out of town. And then again so what? If he cursed me to hell and back at least I'd be with Timmy.

"Ma'am? Um, Izzy?"

I shook my head to clear it and felt it keep shaking. Bad idea. Better hold still.

"I'm sorry. I get a little—distracted since Timmy—since Timmy died. Was there some business you had with Tim I could help you with?"

"Well, I'm not sure. I called to make arrangements — that is, Dr. Guetta asked me to call to say that he'd received the final payment and was ready to ship from our Ithaca office—"

"I'm sorry. The final payment on what?"

"Well, on Dr. Acree's artificial dog."

I smiled and felt my lips keep pulling sideways. Bad idea. Better keep still.

"Let me get this straight. You're saying Timmy ordered an artificial dog from a Dr. Guetta in upstate New York?"

"Uh, yes?" the phone's voice asked, as if it wasn't sure of the right answer, didn't know where my interview was taking it.

"And having received the final payment, this Dr. Guetta is ready to ship the artificial dog to Timmy?"

"Yes?"

Too goddamn late, I'm interested.

Through the gloom, my focus coalesces. The phone's voice becomes a man to me, young and freaked out, a man with a mystery. Paradoxically, just as the voice takes on a shape, it disappears behind a sheath of cotton batting. I hear the trailing last sibilant of the "yes," but it's fuzzy and distant.

Ah hah, I think, so there is a tunnel.

Get straight, I think. Stay conscious. What would Timmy do? I brighten.

"Who made this final payment, if you don't mind my

asking?"

I am listening. The phone's voice replaced with a man, young and freaked out. The man's voice replaced with the sound of riffling papers.

"I'm afraid it doesn't say."

"Does it say *when* the payment was made?"

"It. Why, yes. Huh. This is weird. A bank draft, yesterday, it says."

My heart races. I'm interested. My heart races, quickening blood through every system in my body, and also out every wound. Bad idea. Stay calm. What would Timmy do?

"Listen, Mr.—"

"Goroguchi," he says. "Pudge Goroguchi."

"Pudge Goroguchi. Right. Listen, *Dr.* Goroguchi, is it?"

"Technically, I guess. But just Pudge is fine. Everybody calls me that."

"Okay, listen, Pudge, why don't we go ahead and arrange shipment?"

"Okay, then. I'll set that right up for you, ma'am."

I do not correct him, ask him again to address me as Izzy, although I normally would. His voice is so relieved. He's gained confidence from the elaborate courtesies which run between us. He's gained distance from my stupid, deranging grief.

Lucky him.

I hear his breathing, his pen scratching. I am sitting perfectly still. Airshaft wanders into the room. Looks right at me. Darts away.

Fifteen seconds, maybe twenty have passed. I hear Pudge swallow. His pen is still scratching. A keyboard clicks. An old-fashioned dot matrix printer starts grinding something out. I want to ask him what an artificial dog is. I want to ask. I have to ask. But I'm not asking. Because at the moment not knowing is all I have. I'm not asking because beneath that question, throbbing all through that question, is the other one. The why one. And I'm not asking that. Because at the moment not knowing is all I have. A mystery. In the shape of an angel. In the shape of a man named—

"Hey, Pudge Goroguchi?"

"Still here."

"You have the shipment address right in front of you?"

"33 Howard Street, Apartment 5. New York City."

"Do you think you could have an ambulance sent over here, I mean before you arrange the transfer of Timmy's artificial dog?"

"Right on it," I think he says.

8. Hydraulics

Hairspring ◆ Harsh ◆ He ◆ Heart ◆ Heaven help us ◆ Hides ◆ Hinge ◆ Home ◆ Honorable
Horny ◆ Hospital ◆ Houseplant ◆ Humanity ◆ Huff ◆ Hunk (of bone) ◆ Hydraulics

H is for Hydraulics. I come awake in a hospital, my eyes still closed. I don't want to open them, to look around. By the stinging smells, the tug of tubes on my arms, the numbing pharmaceutical delight of whatever the hell is being pumped into me, the heavy presence of Mark near me, I know where I am. I am in a hospital. I don't need to look at it.

I am in a hospital.

And I'm horny.

I've not wanted sex in a long time now, and it takes me a few seconds longer to realize I'm horny than it does to realize I'm in a hospital. But after all, categorizing the taxonomic vestiges of my humanity is my bag these days, and in the moment between perfectly interspersed beeps on a machine I've not yet seen, I twig to it.

That liquidy tugging in my viscera is unmistakable. I can't say this comes as a surprise to me. Surprise implies expectations—of which I've none, really. But let's say it is unexpected.

I've had sex since Timmy died. If you could call that violent mourning ritual "sex." And most mornings I've masturbated, just purely a matter of hydraulics, a way of getting my blood pressure up, my heart rate going fast enough to haul myself out of bed.

The simple physics of this, the certainty of it, has been a

home to me these past months. Applying pressure to fluid, forcing that fluid through systems in my body, where it acts on other systems. No passion, just hydraulics. Not elegant or romantic or artistic or even interesting.

But a home, and mine.

Hydraulics is one thing though, and actually wanting some is another. Because hydraulics are lovely. Perfectly lovely. No really. The Jersey boys I grew up with, the interesting ones, the ones more likely to trip than swill beer, although of course they swilled their share, all thrilled to hydraulics.

And nature thrills to hydraulics. Well, I guess it makes sense. Spiders and widows. Boxing trainers and starfish and trees. Jersey boys. We've all got a lot of fluid to pump around, and a lot of actions to perform. Adaptively, I guess, the marriage of the two is almost inevitable.

Properly pressurized, properly *harnessed*, fluid'll do almost anything for you, which I guess is why when Blaise Pascal put it all together about hydraulics, he set the world on its goddamn ear, set in motion a whole new way of looking at things, changed everything we think about surfaces, about work, about fluid. And, of course, about pressure.

Could Nature and Blaise Pascal and Jersey boys all be wrong? Of course not. Hydraulics are lovely.

But lust? Lust devoid of hope, lust borne of chaos, without parameters or safety equipment? Lust without function or intent or, my God, even object? Lust is horrible.

My own lust as I lie there is enormous. Oceanic. I can hardly believe how tiny I am in comparison. It buffets me about like so much weightless nothing and I am genuinely startled by my own powerlessness. A monumental force is drowning me and I don't even care.

If you've ever been caught in the curl of a really big wave

and just given yourself over to it because you can do no other, felt the hard slam of the seafloor with gratitude because it heralds the return of normal gravity, you'll know where I'm at with regard to the intensity of my own emotions.

Almost everything is wrong with me, but I am not stupid. Obviously my deranging lust must somehow be allied to my deranging grief. I suppose it is even possible that my deranging lust *is* my deranging grief, costumed by my head in attire not entirely inappropriate to my hospital sojourn.

I keep my eyes closed a moment longer, fearing Mark's hard face peering at me, measuring me for health and for contrition. Fearing he would look at me and know. Fearing he would know my lust and mistake it for a sign of life.

Mark tells me he wants me to find a way to live. He berates me about it. Berates and cajoles and begs until I want to scream at him to shut up and usually do. But the hard truth is nothing short of throwing myself onto the pyre would've really satisfied either of us.

That is our secret shame, which keeps us together and fighting. That he feels as I do. That I'd better serve Timmy dead. It seems harsh, I know, but in principle, I can't really kick against Mark's most secret wishes. I'm not offended by the idea of treating myself like an old-fashioned widow, burying myself with Timmy as a sign of my devotion, and so he'll have someone to rub his feet and feed him grapes in the next life. And so no one else can have me.

I don't mind the plan which thrums in Mark's dark heart in theory. In fact, I'd prefer it. But in my entire life I only ever set about acting in behest of one other person's deepest heart. Timmy. And look where it got me.

So I guess I'm biding my time.

"Izzy," he says, and I open my eyes to meet his sand-clear

ones, raw and red-rimmed.

He coughs. Hides his face in his hands. Gets a good honest glare on.

"Izzy," he says, "there's someone waiting to see you."

"That's all? No 'You're okay. You're in a hospital. You had a miscarriage and they say you're badly malnourished. But all you need is rest?' No 'lookatcha, Kid, you're a mess?' No 'I blame myself?'"

He blinks at me.

"What, Mark? Does that about sum it up?"

"There's someone waiting to see you."

With every fiber of my being not actively engaged in engorging my vulva, I resist the urge to ask if it's Timmy. This is the obvious line, and the dumbest one, and I've only given up life, not discernment. Not *taste*. I'm after something slightly less crass. I'm after something *reasonable*.

But when you resist the urge to say what you mean, a deeper truth, the one you didn't care to share, the one you didn't even know you meant, generally falls out of your mouth. Or so I used to observe.

"Is it an entomologist?" I ask.

"Sure and how would I know that, lass?"

"Well, is it a lass?"

He sighs quietly, runs his huge hand through his bristly black and gray hair. His gesture's meaning is apparent: this hunk of bone, this smear of ash, this unholy slip of a girl is now my lot in life. Well, I guess I mean his gesture's meaning is apparent to me because so much of this brute's body language is Timmy's.

Besides, I have to live with myself too. And I know it isn't fun.

"It's a vodka martini drinker," he says at last.

"You can tell that by looking at someone?"

Mark ignores this. He leans over the bed's railing, his glare is good and hardened now. He sniffs and he knows. He smells it on me. As simple as that. My God, what stupid shambling simians we all are.

"He's pacing out there."

"Pacing," I say. "He."

"Do you know what you're doing, girl?"

I prop myself up on my elbows, pulling away from the white, white linen.

"Shit, Mark. Do I *look* like I know what I'm doing?"

He squats beside my hospital bed, his face right next to mine, touches my cheek with his knuckles.

"I'm after worrying about me brother's memory. Can you understand that, girl?"

I refrain from mentioning that he's had me himself. He's so close I can hear his big ape heart thumping, see the artery in his throat pulsing out the four-stroke beat of a heat engine. More hydraulics at work here, pumping tears out the flat yellow eyes in his battered face.

I do not cry myself, because I do not cry anymore. Instead, I have acquired at each hinge of my jaw a hard knot of muscle and scar tissue, cartilage and burnt-out nerves; two tough lumps of pus and sinew and suppressed crying jags.

I do not cry anymore because past a certain point, my own tears began to bore me. But the mechanics of Mark's tears I easily recognize. The mechanics I can identify with. The mechanics, so to speak, *move* me.

Once I was a hairspring, an endless plane of coiled possibility, fixed at one end so the other could scream in the stars. It was only when the fixed end hurled itself into an airshaft that I became such a sullen, lifeless ass.

"I can tell you exactly what Timmy'd say, Mark. But I don't

think it's going to help you any."

Mark stands from his crouch. He gestures, rolling with his massive taped wrist: out with it, then.

"He'd say it's nothing. Just nature's way of reminding us she loves a mixture. He'd say if I actually had any goddamn purpose in life he could advise me to sublimate. Then he'd smile wickedly and allow as how he supposed if I was going to be such a bore about it, I'd just have to bring the lust to bed with us, and visit it upon him."

I prop myself up further, and pin Mark's wet eyes.

"But by then I'd feel so much more alive from that thirty second chat with Timmy than I ever did the rest of my life put together that the crush would be gone anyway."

I sit all the way up, straining a tube which is pumping fresh fluid into my body. Using hydraulics. Mark stands and his eyes are streaming.

"Heaven help us, lass. That is *just* what he'd say, isn't it?"

"If he weren't dead, Mark."

He moves toward the door. Outside it is the world. I can still push this either way.

I strain against my lifelines, unhappy in my lust. I suspect it stems from some primitive survival instinct, the kind of immutable force which acts upon us from the inside out. The kind of survival instinct which will not yield to reason.

Timmy had a riotous assortment of houseplants. Richly red-shot coleus, mostly. And preposterous elephant-eared ivy and pots and pots of chive which he put in everything he ate. He was forever cutting them back, and then leaving them to root in my beer glasses.

Right after he died, I passed the time watching them die too. When it was absolutely clear to the plants that no more light or water would be forthcoming, they bloomed obscenely. Crazy lilac flowers bursting with cheap perfume. They looked—and smelled—like hundreds of little hookers. The houseplants knew they were done for, but were unable to go out with any grace. Instead they kicked up a last-ditch effort to get a little something going in the pollination department.

I hope this isn't what I'm up to. Mark's hand is on the knob. He is looking to me for instructions. I can still push this either way.

My lust is all for beckoning the entomologist to my hospital bed and having him right there. I do not care about the morality of the situation one way or the other. I'm way beyond all that, out on a goddamn limb.

But if I allow the strange boy pacing outside my hospital room to pretend to himself that his motives are entirely honorable, that's he's come all the way down here just to see if I am okay, that this is something any human would do for another, he will want to save me.

And I do not want to be saved. I do not want to be thought of as salvageable. I want only to destroy my own humanity, to suffocate each of my emotions with a precise label—until I have no emotions left. And then to die quietly, leaving no traces, and certainly no riotous blossoms.

Besides, I don't think I could get off with someone who wanted to save me. That's a kid's game, really, and I was way over it even before my heart blew out. Back when I liked it at all, I liked it on the sad side of rough, with a goodly dose of black humor.

Back when I liked it at all. When I liked it. Way back when then. When. It all liked at I when back. Liked I back all when at it. All when I liked it at back.

"Will you tell him I'm not up to company. But he could bring the artificial dog down to the Howard Street place. In about three weeks?"

Mark turns his back to me. His shoulder blades are eloquent. His frustration with me is his greatest intensity. In all my self-obsessed meanderings I'd kind of forgotten that he obviously had his own plans for the artificial dog or he wouldn't have made the final payment.

He turns and takes a gulp of air and lets it out his nose in a long huff. He smiles crookedly and so so gently, then gestures with his crazy Irish eyebrows, Timmy's eyebrows: get a look at yourself; you're a mess.

"Better make it four, Kid."

"Okay. Four."

"I'll check on you later," he says.

9. IMMOLATOR.

I'm (a maggot) ◆ Idiosyncratic ◆ Ignore ◆ Immolator ◆ Inadequate ◆ Ingenuous ◆ Initial
Instar ◆ Interstate ◆ Introducing (Mr. Click) ◆ Irate ◆ Irish ◆ Irrational

I is for Immolator. Among the staff of Stock Transfer Complaints Defects Correspondents in the Tenders and Exchanges Department of the Interstate Bank of New York and New Jersey, I am known as an Immolator.

Most people in this line of work get frustrated if they have to stray too far from our set of ten or twelve boilerplate response letters. So if crazy cousin Nancy and her hippie lawyer want to challenge the transfer of shares after Grandma Abby's death, that's no problem. Change a few words on Stock Transfer Complaint Letter Number Three, personalize the mother, and you're good to go. Or if you need to guarantee the signature of someone suddenly transferring all their assets to a girl called Nicole Pasties, c/o General Delivery, Las Vegas, then Stock Transfer Complaint Letter Number Eight is your baby.

But every couple of weeks or so, a stock transfer complaint will come in which is, well, insane. These complaints need to be made to disappear, to go up in a puff of smoke, and since each instance of stock transfer insanity is perforce idiosyncratic, there are no boilerplate response letters to be had. Thus, most Tenders and Exchanges Departments have someone like me, in our argot, an Immolator.

I sat at my cubicle all morning, working through the

mountain of crazy letters which had piled up in my absence. The people working around me were all too stupid or too selfish to be earnest with me, or even solicitous, and I was grateful. I am hopelessly heartsore and perplexed, as a permanent state of being. Talking about it doesn't help.

All I wanted was to do my work, clock out and get home in time to deal with Airshaft and the fleas. All I wanted was to clean the place up enough to make room for the artificial dog. All I wanted was to get home in time to make sure I didn't look like a snake-haired widder-woman when Pudge Goroguchi got there. I was afraid if he thought I was too messed up, he wouldn't let me have the artificial dog, whatever it was.

All I wanted was to get my hands on the artificial dog.

The first three letters on my stack were all of a stripe, possessed of the kind of regional resentment characterized by the phrase "Interstate Bank of Jew York and Jew Jersey," a pun that's apparently dear to the hearts of Plains states paranoiacs. Anyhow, I see it a lot.

I dispatched those in short order, following my own cardinal rules for such correspondence. Don't insult 'em. Find something to respond to. Ignore the manifesto.

As I reached for the fourth letter, which was printed on smeary purple mimeograph sheets, and scrawled over with what I was hoping was brown crayon, my extension lit up. Answering the phone at the Immolator desk is always a risky business. I try my damnedest to write responses that will send the complainers away forever, mollified if not satisfied, but dealing with the Mad isn't always so straightforward, as I've learned from Mark's intense Irish face, now that I've apparently joined their ranks.

The people on the other end of the phone are often irate, and almost always irrational, and every once in a while they become so unhinged that I'm forced to take an action which will almost certainly set them to pestering the higher-ups. Because of this, it is a dangerous action for our entire department, and I employ it as sparingly as possible. It goes a little something like this:

". . . (increasingly shrill) In that case, Madam, you are hereby notified of pending full disownment and divorcement and full damages suit. Acting as Kaiser, I will remove you from all lines of lineage to me in the seeking of leniency from me—"

"Okay, Mrs. Imbrie, I can hear that you're pretty upset. Here's what I think we should—"

"(screaming) Don't interrupt me! You are an evil being and I, a powerful ruler. Gentle and forgiving I was, but no longer—"

"I'm sorry to hear that, Mrs. Imbrie. But to get back to your question about—"

"(hysterical) Sodomist! Gin Imbiber! Oedopexer!"

"You know what, Mrs. Imbrie? I think you might be on to something here. Maybe you should explain this to my supervisor. He's a lot more knowledgeable than I am about this, uh, kind of situation. Mrs. Imbrie? Allow me to introduce you to Mr. Click."

And with that, you simply hang up. And await the shitstorm from the executive suite.

I put off answering the call for nine or ten buzzes, my finger resting on the lit button. I didn't want to have to introduce anyone to Mr. Click my first day back in three months. But I didn't want to slack off, either.

"Good morning," I said into the headset, finally, "Interstate."

"Hi, uh. May I please speak to Ms. Oytsershifl?"

"Pudge Goroguchi. Hi. You're not backing out on me, I hope."

"No. I, I just wanted to make sure we were still on for tonight. I'm driving down."

"Far as I know, we're still on."

"Right. Good. I. Uh."

I breathed slowly, fighting back panic. I winged a piece of balled-up legal paper at the fat man in the cubicle across from me. He looked up from a monstrously dog-eared volume of Gibbon. I gestured to him to throw me the box of latex gloves, which he did, laughing. Good arm on that guy, I thought. I breathed slowly, preternaturally, seconds mounting. I put a glove on my left hand and touched the brown smear on the fourth letter, caressed it. Crayon.

Still, it's good to be careful. A letter like that could easily be coated with a killing dose of PCP. Or worse. A crazy letter can explode like a little bomb in your life. A crazy person can explode like a little bomb in someone's life. A crazy person, exploding like a little bomb, can ruin her own chances at getting her hands on an artificial dog. A crazy person has to be careful.

"You know I don't know what I'm doing, don't you, Pudge Goroguchi?" I said into the headset, calmly.

"You mean with the artificial dog?"

"I mean I'm so full of rage and pain that that's all I am anymore, okay? I can't be expected to act honorably, is what I mean."

"Well, geez."

He puffed out the words, yet with a tone so ingenuous I had to laugh. And something in my laugh transformed us both.

"Well, you know, I'm just an entomologist."

"I know."

"No, what I mean is, I'm just an entomologist. I probably can't help you with the pain. But, uh, I'm young and athletic. Maybe I can do something about that rage for you."

This struck me as quite possibly the most heroic thing anyone had ever said to me. I didn't want to blow it. We breathed quietly for another moment. And retreated to a safe distance.

Careful.

"Yeah. Okay. That'd be cool. I guess we'll see."

"Yeah. Okay. So, depending on the traffic on the interstate, I'll be there around eight?"

We hung up. I mean, talk about introducing someone to Mr. Click.

REF: SMITHY0.TNE

April 26, 2011

Crazy Eyes and Dank
212 24th Street, First Floor
Brooklyn, NY 11232
RE: Rehupa Financial Corporation
A/C: Crazy Eyes and Dank

Dear Sirs:

We are returning the enclosed Transmittal Form and certificates #43315 and #38505 as an inadequate basis for the exchange of your Rehupa Financial Corporation Common Stock. Please resubmit these items with the additional requirement specified below:

In order for us to comply with your special instructions, the signatures "Crazy Eyes" and "Dank" must be guaranteed by a commercial bank, trust company, member firm of a major stock exchange, or similar institution participating in the Security Transfer Association's MEDALLION Program. No other means of signature verification is valid in this context.

[& certainly not a scrawled note from the goddamned Mexican horse doctor who sold you the drugs that prompted your desire to change your names in the first

place, you dumb sons of bitches.]

Should you require any additional information from the Interstate Bank of New York and New Jersey, please feel free to contact one of our representatives at the telephone number indicated above.

Sincerely,

Authorized Signature (Izzy Oytsershifl)
Tenders and Exchange Department
DOTS: 9172421339

REF #: COMJONES12.TNE

April 26, 2011

RE: Communipaw Bancorp (unexchanged Bancshares of Communipaw)
A/C: Glen and Baby Doll Jones

Dear Mr. and Mrs. Jones:

Enclosed please find certificates #20120 and #09368 representing two (2) of the five (5) shares of Bancshares of Communipaw Common Stock which remain outstanding in your account. Please resubmit these two certificates with the Affidavit of Loss Form which you will soon receive from our Lost Securities Department.

The completed and notarized Affidavit of Loss will serve as a substitute for your missing three shares and enable us to redeem all five.

[Please note that it is the considered opinion of my colleagues here at the Tenders and Exchanges Department that none of the preceding will be in the least bit intelligible to a pair of apoplectic Jersey crackers such as yourselves.

*The fact that you managed to hold onto the two above enclosed
extant shares by stashing them within the body cavities of the no
doubt unusually endowed Mrs. Jones does not, as you indicated in
your initial correspondence, strike us as "quick thinking," so much
as creepy and sick-making. Even if we had been impressed with this
girlie-show stunt, without a completed and notarized Affidavit of
Loss Form, our hands are, so to speak, tied.]*

Should you require any further assistance, please feel free to
contact one of our representatives at the telephone number
indicated above.

Sincerely,
Authorized Signature (Izzy Oytsershifl)
Tenders and Exchanges Department
DOTS: 7183692829

My mind was not on my work. My mind was on the
maggots. They sat all around me, doing their stupid work, the
work I seem to be too crazy to do anymore. They sat all around
me, doing their work, drooling their lost dreams. Maggots, the
squirming, dead-thing-chomping stage of a fly's life.

Maggots molt twice before they get around to turning into
flies. These three, soft-bodied, larval epochs are called instars. At
each stage instar, a maggot lacerates the rotting tissue of the dead
thing with its mouth hook, and spits an enzyme into the cut-up
flesh. The enzyme reduces the tissue to an ooze, which the maggot
then slurps up. Lots of maggots make lots of ooze, so maggots
congregate in clumps and move en masse through the corpse in
question. This is pragmatism on their part, rather than brotherly
love, although maggot masses are most often borne of eggs from
the same hatching.

Each instar of a maggot is bigger than the next and eats
more. Maggots are white and slimy and segmented and have

mouth hooks and spit flesh-dissolving enzymes and move in clumps. Maggots keep doing what they do, even though they must know they are essentially horrific. Maggots squirm.

Maggots are gross. Even I, a rationalist, a creature of science, the only girl who ever let Timmy feed his fleas on my arm (and once my thigh), admit this. Maggots are gross.

But maggots are pragmatists.

One time Daffy Duck, as he went about saving his own duck's ass, leaving Bugs hanging, turned to the camera and said "okay, I'm a louse, but I'm a live louse."

Say it with me. Okay, I'm a louse but I'm a live louse. Say it with me. I'm a live louse. I'm Daffy Duck. I'm a pragmatist. Say it with me.

I'm a maggot.

10. JANGLE

(Io)Jack ◆ Jackass Gentrification ◆ Jangle ◆ Jawbone ◆ Jello Biafra ◆ Jersey Jew ◆ Johnny Thunders ◆ Jolt ◆ Jowly ◆ Jumped ◆ Just (long enough)

J is for Jangle. A city block has a melodic line. A tone. A *mode*. If you've lived on it for fifteen years, as I have lived on crooked Howard Street, its rhythms are so internal as to be part of you. Even if you live in a back apartment, against a side street, facing an airshaft, as I have for ten of those fifteen years, you are part of the composition. A long external change, such as the jackass gentrification of the neighborhood, amounts to nothing more than a variation on your block's particular theme.

But anything small and sudden, like a tourist-friendly, horse-mounted cop making his way down the block, disrupts that steady flow. Anything small and sudden, like Timmy landing in the airshaft, jangles the air up and down the street. You feel it in your body.

You feel it in your body. A jolt of trepidation. Awareness. Spider-sense alarm. As if you're watching an old silent oater and the in-house pianist suddenly breaks into "Injuns are Coming" music, banging out bare fifths over and over again with his left hand, playing anything at all with his right. But you don't hear it. You don't see it. You feel it in your body.

So I felt it before I heard it, felt it as I sat in the apartment, staring gloomily at the stucco walls, gulping water and aspirin. A stirring in the ether, a change in my block's familiar dissonance. I jumped to the window and then I heard it. A lion's dragstrip roar, unmistakable, a factory-installed 426 HEMI engine—endemic to my Jersey childhood, absurd on a crooked street on the outskirts of Chinatown.

I felt it before I heard it and I heard it before I saw it and I was downstairs on the stoop just as it screeched to a halt in front of me. A '71 Road Runner, show-room perfect, lime green with a black vinyl top. The pop-up Air Grabber had a shark's face decal.

Everything stopped. The block's music . . . stopped. The guys from the Algo Dye Works materialized outside their shop. A face appeared in every window like cartoon mice in swiss cheese. A blonde woman with a cell phone froze in mid-squawk. A dead ringer for Jello Biafra dropped his forty on the sidewalk. Uncle Willy standing next to me held Fuz back as if from temptation, as if from the gates of hell. Fuz's mouth hung so far open I feared his jawbone would crack.

And then Mr. Sing, the ten-thousand year-old herbalist laughed and went back into his storefront. And the block's melodic line reasserted itself. And a tall, impossibly exotic looking guy emerged from the driver's side door. Tall, vaguely Asian features, glasses, no kidding, cracked through one lens, farm-fresh hair. Pudge Goroguchi.

"Hey," I said. "I had a dream about that car."

He chuckled. The easy laugh of a man who knows his car's a heart-breaker.

"Hey," he said, "only one?"

He came around the car to shake my hand, his left leg limping and shaking. The dance of a leg which has been working a beartrap-sprung Hurst-4 clutch all the way from Ithaca and then through the stop-go-curse traffic of New York, New York.

He caught my look and reached back to open the passenger door.

"I take your point, but this is an original, 2009 model, hand-built artificial dog. One of twenty-two known to exist. Only fifty generations of fleas on it. Should I have brought it in a four-door?"

We struggled the components of the artificial dog up the tenement stairs. The main body of the artificial dog was a clear acrylic cube, about a foot and half long on each side. Within the cube were twenty-five aluminum cylinders each of which bottomed out into a plastic dish. At the cube's side was a small electric space heater. We also carried a cooler, a tiny incubator and something that looked like a wigged-out Dust Buster. I regret to report the artificial dog did not look like any dog I had ever seen.

We came through the open apartment door. Pudge Goroguchi made straight for Timmy's flea tanks. I peered in the cooler. Bags of blood. And cans of dog food.

Pudge Goroguchi came back in the room. His eyes were wide.

"You've got some beauties back there," he said.

I held a can of dog food aloft.

"It runs on dog food, like a real dog?"

He laughed and moved closer to me, took the can out of my hands.

"It runs on electricity and human precision. The dog food's for the larvae."

"It's not what I expected," I said.

He shook his head sadly.

"No. It never is. It's a pimped-out acrylic cube, hella conducive to flea-breeding. But we needed the catchy name, to seduce the dimwits at the pest-control companies. I brought you this, though."

A dog decal. Like Scooby-Doo but pink and slathering with red devil-eyes. A dog sticker from a supermarket gum ball machine. He slapped it on the side of the artificial dog.

"Am I?" he said.

I hadn't thought about it yet.

Until this moment, I hadn't thought about it. I bluff for time, studying him.

"Why? Did you bring a sticker for yourself too?"

His laugh is real, his eyes black and gleamy. His dishwater blond Midwestern boy hair looks like a wig. "Pudge" is obviously some vestige of school-boy nickname. There's a big gap in his teeth I instantly want to get my tongue into. He is quite young. He can't be thirty. His body is effortlessly fit, without being, as they say, sculpted. A working guy's body. All flat square planes, sheaths of sheetrock dusty hard muscle moving easily under his clothes. Like Mark's body. Like old Coogan's alcoholic body. Like Timmy's body. Well, you know. *Before*.

Boys like this always seem to coalesce around me, as if there were a caste system. I mean, how do you even *meet* a neurasthenic scion? Or a jowly son of the tonier burbs? A proud State Senator's only boy?

When I was sixteen, I worked at the Haunted Mansion at Long Branch. We rotated positions frequently. There were no steady roles. But what I liked best was to sit in the Headless Man rig and watch them come through in the tunnel's ceiling mirror. The keg-shined frat boys. The larval bankers I'd end up catching flak for. Their arms around squealing big-haired Jersey Girls from my own school district. Watch them and wonder. How do you even *meet* a guy a like that?

But, shit. Why would you want to, right?

Pudge Goroguchi takes my silent class-ruminations for approval. Or maybe it's my feet moving closer to him he takes as approval. We move together through the apartment, toward the flea tanks which he stares at in wonder.

"What part of this is about Timmy for you?" I ask.

My voice doesn't sound like the me in my head. My voice is breathless rather than grave. My voice is a big-haired squealing Jersey Girl. He laughs.

"Oh, only ten percent or so. His thesis is my favorite book. I keep it on my bed stand, so of course that makes me jealous. Mine is all graphs and math and engineering specs. But he spent a small fortune on the artificial dog which I helped design. So that kind of makes him my bitch, right?"

He laughs again.

"What part of this is about hurting Dr. Acree for you," he says, pressing my body against the wall next to the flea tanks.

The first question anyone has asked me in months that I feel I can answer honestly. The first question anyone has asked me in what seems like forever which I find erotic.

And I am moved to tears that even now, even saying what he's saying, doing what he's doing, he calls Timmy "Dr. Acree."

"I don't know," I breathe out when I can, "probably all of it."

"Then you're not really in a position to talk, are you?"

I am not, as it happens, in a position to talk. Because his body is on my body, his hand is on my mouth. We are against the wall.

He is, as promised, athletic. And what excites me is not the friction of his cock as it moves against the nerves in my cunt or his hammer thumb on my clitoris, but the force of his body as it slams into mine, just as hatefully as if he could read my mind.

These slams I count. There are 538 of them. And as the numbers mount, I feel for just a moment lighter. As if some—not all but some—of the rage has been squeezed out of me.

If you were wondering about sex in hell, this is sex in hell. Not Dante's writhing pits of overworked burning nerves, fused together for all eternity, slick with regret. Sex in hell brings not pleasure but the absence of pain, just long enough to shake off some of the numbing complacency. Just long enough to make us realize how much pain we're actually in, to make us feel its weight and sting anew.

When Timmy was my model it wasn't easy to strive for decency, but I always tried. But after he betrayed that role and behaved indecently himself, well, with Timmy gone, I can't believe how easy it is to be stupid and cruel. What it seems no one can possibly understand, because, I mean, how could they, is that with Timmy gone the way he went, I am not just a woman in grief.

I am an apostate. *An Meshumed*, as we say in Yiddish.

Faithless. This is not a normal state of being for a thirty-four year old Jew from Bloomfield, New Jersey. It's Indian Country. Hear those open fifths? The relentless, primitive Tom-Tom beat? That's the warning. The Injuns are coming. All that you've lived by *does not apply here.*

But not entirely faithless. I have one faith left. Reason. And until Reason hands me my ass, as it will sooner or later, I am sticking with it.

"Do you have a LoJack on that thing," I ask as he dresses.

"Are you kidding? Wire my ride into the cops? No LoJack. No car alarm. And no insurance company will touch it for less than my entire annual salary."

"What is it about you flea scientists that make you so goddamn sure of yourselves?"

Again he laughs. Again. This boy is so good-humored he defies all reason.

"You want me to leave you instructions for the 'dog? Or come back and show you how it's done?"

"Both," says the squealing big-haired Jersey girl who has seized control of my tongue.

Neither. But I'm not going to tell the co-inventor of the artificial dog that I want one around just as a fetish item. It would be rude. And a boy whose good humor defies all Reason is the last thing I need.

I have no intention of raising *more* fleas. Keeping alive the ones I've already *got* is killing me. Then again, maybe it's not such a bad idea. If some fleas are killing me, more might polish me off.

And, if I get the last thing I need, I'll be free to go.

I go down with him to say goodbye. To touch the car. It kicks over like something out of a dream. A dream in which the only guy who ever really lit you up is leaving you for Johnny Thunders.

"Know why flea scientists are so confident?" he asks under the ground-shaking bone-quaking raw roaring noise.

"No. Why?"

"It's the fleas, Ma'am."

K.O. ◆ Kaddish ◆ Kansas ◆ Keel ◆ Keen ◆ Keep (the Faith) ◆ Kelvin
Kerplunk ◆ Kicking ◆ Kill ◆ Kiss me ◆ Kleptomaniac ◆ Knee

K is for *Kaddish*. I have not said a *Kaddish* for Timmy yet, and if I haven't said one yet, I don't think I'm going to. Nobody's asked me about this, because I don't seem to know any Jews anymore, but if someone had asked me, I'd planned to say that it wouldn't mean anything to Timmy. This isn't strictly true, because Timmy was a big drama queen and a ritual freak, was helpless with merriment whenever I cursed in Yiddish. In fact, he probably would've dug it. But I am not expecting any arguments to come from that quarter.

Instead I was thinking of the Rabbi of my youth. If the Rabbi of my youth should come up to me on the street—but no. Scratch that. If the Rabbi of my youth came up to me on the street, I'd know him instantly by his smug beatific expression and kleptomaniac wife in Mamie Eisenhower drag. I'd know him instantly. And I'd run.

But I wouldn't know a modern Rabbi if one came up to me and bit me on the knee. If one came up to me, a good, modern one who'd minored in Cultural Anthropology, I wouldn't know him from a beat cop. And I wouldn't have time to run. Or I couldn't. Because of the injury to my knee.

Anyway, I suppose a guy like that would tell me that you don't do it for the Dead, you do it for yourself. Say the *Kaddish*, I mean. And of course I have a whole arsenal of reasons why I don't care to coat myself in soothing rituals should I ever get into that conversation—leading with, maybe *you* do it for yourself, *Rebbe*, but these are not my people.

Even if they are.

The truth is more raw than that, I'm afraid. More raw. More basic. More primitive. And more tedious. I can't say the *Kaddish* because the *Kaddish*, whatever its ritual uses, is, in its essence, a hymn in praise of God.

I do not believe in God, and if I did, I'd probably be ready to kill God right about now. Praising him? Praising hymn praising him? Well, now. That would be a pretty hollow joke.

It is said that we kill the Gods when we stop believing in them. And if that's the case, then I've already done my part with regard to God. But I do not worship at the altar of a God, have not for years, was only going through the motions then.

My great belief—apart from reason which fails me even as I cling to it, like a junkie boyfriend—my great belief has been in my love for Timmy. I have faith in our love, Tim's and mine, but Timmy is dead—and by his own hand—anyway.

We kill our Gods when we stop believing in them, but we cannot keep love alive by believing in it. So, I'm forced to conclude that though both involve faith, which defies reason, love and religion are not allied disciplines. Which leads me back to Reason. Which is failing me even as I cling to it. Like a junkie boyfriend.

Reason does not involve faith, except I guess that to believe in it, you are willingly choosing a belief system that is an imperfect instrument for navigating the treacherous shoals of the human heart. But reason, logic, science, these disciplines I cling to.

Reason is good. Reason is my friend. To use it, to exercise my faith in it, I keep arguing with my favorite straw man, the modern Rabbi. Straw Rabbi, like Br'er Rabbit, is so innocent, and so devious at once, he enrages me.

Straw Rabbi say: you do not have to stop loving someone, stop believing in your love, just because he is dead. And to that I wanna reply this:

Timmy went kerplunk.

Timmy checked out. Timmy opted for the big K.O. Timmy could not have loved me, believed in our love, and also killed himself. If Timmy did not love me, did not believe in our love, then our love wasn't really there. Just as Timmy is not. Not really there. Here. And yet I keep loving him, believing in that love.

Straw Rabbi say: keep the Faith. I say: Timmy went Kerplunk. We could go on forever like that. Straw Rabbi stuck to Tar Baby. Forever. At a fucking crossroads.

But having applied that mythology, I reject it. I don't have any use for Southern folklore just as I don't have any use for Judaism. If I think I am looking to them, I am clearly not thinking clearly.

There are fallacies here too numerous to count. Fallacies and bad ideas and ill winds and hypotheses built on sand and conclusions drawn on bad samples and margins of error as wide as the great outdoors. Or at least Kansas.

K is for Kansas, which I keep calling Pudge Goroguchi. Because that's where he's from, and that's how tough kids from New Jersey talk. At least in the movies. We call people by where they're from. K is for Kansas which I call Pudge Goroguchi when I think of him. To remind me that that's where he's from. To remind me that his world is not my world. To remind me that he walks in light.

How else can I put it without sounding too stupid? He belongs. He's part of the flow. Light and joy and fun dance off his shambling bulk and in their aura, my own body lightens, almost literally. As if I can feel its core filling with helium.

But this is just a parlor trick of Physics. Darkness absorbs light. Blackness is its absence. And Kansas, man? His world is not my world. If I let myself forget that I'm a shadow, I'm afraid I will swallow him whole.

But here I am ignoring the very nature of the spectrum. More drama. Useless grappling after order. Kicking against entropy. Sloppy thinking. To call this thinking Physics is to insult Physics. Physics takes it up the ass, I'm saying. Physics blows sailors. Physics wears combat boots.

Physics' mama.

Spectroscopy tells us that where helium is a large presence in a star's atmosphere, as in the blue-white b-type Milky Way stars like Rigel, it makes its presence known by absorbing particular wavelengths. This absorption in turn creates lines of darkness in the spectrum corresponding to the wavelengths emitted by the vapors of helium. If helium is placed between a prism and a source of light which emits all the wavelengths, these dark streaks appear. It was in fact these dark streaks in the full spectrum of light from the sun which led to the discovery of helium, hence the name helium, derived from *helios*, the Greek sun.

All of which is to say that if there are dark streaks appearing in Pudge Goroguchi, they are his own damn business. And if the atmosphere around him lends me a buoyancy, a certain familiar squeakiness of voice, I suppose that burden is mine. Or that's what Physics would have me believe.

K is for Kiss me, Kansas, words which my tongue forms behind my teeth, over and over like a mantra. Words which my tongue forms but I don't say. Words which my tongue forms behind my teeth even as my heart longs for you, Timmy. I don't say them, these words. Because my heart belongs with you, Timmy. In the world of shadows.

But never mind that. Helium be damned. Here we are concerned with K. What does Spectroscopy tell us about K-type stars like Pollux? They are cool, well, relatively so, clocking in at an average temperature of 4250 degrees Kelvin. They look orange. The dark bands in their spectrum indicate lots of neutralized metals, and calcium, both neutralized and ionized. And, blissfully, there seems to be absolutely nothing about K-type stars that is germane to my situation.

There is no metaphor here. My brain bounces around frantically, searching for something outside myself, something cold, codified, reasonable. Searching for answers? Well yeah, I can't deny that I'm doing this. But too, I am searching for surcease, for some system it is impossible to have an egotistical take on. Someplace where there is meaning, but where me, and the stupid death of my soul, have no resonance.

For a moment, reflecting on the impossibly distant orange dwarves which have absolutely nothing the fuck to do with me, I think I have it, the ease of non-being. The peace Timmy must have. A moment, and then it's gone.

Pollux is a K-type star.

Pollux.

Pollux and not Castor.

And we're off again. Me and Straw Rabbi, that smiling, bearded expert on cultural relativism. He smiles, plucks an egg sandwich out of his long, Times Square gag-shop beard. An egg and cheese sandwich. On a roll. With Taylor Ham. He holds it away from his body with barely disguised disgust, as if this *treyf* didn't in fact spring from his body, wasn't stashed in his goddamn beard. As if he is innocent of it. Although I wonder how much forbidden pig actually makes it into that fruit roll-up mystery meat, First Food of New Jersey.

I am riveted by his hypocrisy, my eyes on the egg sandwich. Meanwhile, he is talking, reminding me that Castor and Pollux are twinned only in our imagination. That even binary star systems are a construct, a perception, one way of looking at things.

In Aztec Astronomy (Astronomy, yes, and not Astrology — I may have lost my mind, but I haven't yet replaced it with oatmeal), Gemini is a ball court. A ball court. Like Giant Stadium. Like the Meadowlands. Wimbledon. Fenway. Like Shea was once. The Springdale Park basketball hangout in East Orange, New Jersey.

Gemini is a ball court. On it, the ruler of the night Black Tezcatlipoca presides over a game which determines the fate of man. And the fate of each man.

What happened in that game, I wonder, to take my Timmy from me? To send my Timmy on a gainer? Did Quetzalcoatl score? Did Tlaloc throw a spitter? Or so I would wonder, if I were an Aztec farmer, or a sacrificial virgin, instead of a Jew from Bloomfield, New Jersey with too wide a pool of general knowledge. Neither sacrificed nor a virgin. And not even a cultural relativist.

Clearly, as I say, I am not thinking clearly. This much is clear: my grief has deranged me. Split me into two camps. Inside me contend a keen like a sonic boom, and a survival instinct, a self-correcting keel. A keen and a keel.

The keel, by its nature, seeks after balance. Balance. Reason. Science. Hard fact. The death of emotion. Hovering at zero. Even. Neutral. Oblivion.

The keen longs to make itself heard. To have its screeches scream for redress, stretch forever, sear into the darkest night, into the endlessly reduplicating backwaters, 'til it can be heard in every shit-kicker cowboy town at the ass-end of the cosmos. The ass-ends of the cosmos. Oblivion also.

Two poles, keen and keel. Between them, ridiculous to me, I am still alive.

12. LEAP

Ladder ◆ Landing ◆ Laser Eye Surgery ◆ Lass ◆ Last Judgement
Lateral ◆ Laugh ◆ Leap ◆ Lets Loose ◆ Life's Blood ◆ (De Valera's) Limp
Lintel ◆ Loneliness ◆ Loved ◆ Lufkin 100 ft. Tape Measure ◆ Lurching

L is for Leap. The Balustrade, I think we would all agree, is a stupid name for a bar. Timmy hated it and in his darkest moods, which were of course not dark at all, he'd refer to his father's bar as Paddy's. Timmy's father (not named Paddy) also hated it. Even Mark hates it. But "The Balustrade" came to the former owner in a dream and none of the Acrees were willing to mess with *that* mojo. Swooning sentimental fools, the lot of them.

The original sign, weather-beaten and indecipherable, hangs from an upstairs lintel on heavy rusted chains. Or it did. For emerald-swathed decade upon decade. Over the original wooden door. Outshone by the neon "BAR" sign. Outshone by seagull droppings and later crack vials on the cobble beneath it. A mousy, unlovely little thing, as relics go.

And as relics go, it went.

Tonight, as I approached the bar, Mark was up on a ladder, ripping the thing down. His face was determined, but it almost always is. His face was maniacal. And that was new.

"What the hell you doin', boy?"

He flew down the ladder, kissed the top of my head, broke the sign over his knee, and tossed the halves into the street. I looked at him, at them. Even up close, the letters, burned into the wood with a hot iron sometime during the Boss Tweed era, were unreadable.

"Ain't you got a little basin of the Upper New York Bay around here someplace you could toss that in?"

"Indeed I do, and 'tis not far. Come on."

He scooped the broken pieces up with one hand, in one motion, and handed me a half, then took off running to the end of the street where the ripe green water lapped against a pier older than the sign. I followed, flung my piece in after his. Looked at him.

"So," I said, "what are you gonna call the bar?"

He grinned, then jogged easily back to the ladder, where he perched, still grinning, as I walked toward him.

"Come in for a jar, Izzy. I'll tell you all about it. Or did you want to work the other side of the stick tonight?"

"Both. Either. Why are you grinning like that?"

He chuckled, bounded off the ladder, held the door with a flourish.

There were hipsters in the bar. Young, aggressively eccentric, no black leather or tiny glasses or cell phones. And certainly no *gelt* to speak of. Not the monied fools choking every alley in Manhattan. But bonafide hipsters nonetheless, whose presence presaged the flow of money sure as the Last Judgement.

A short boy with an impossible mop of shaggy red hair was explaining Lacan to Boris. Four preposterously pretty girls, one from each corner of the globe, black, white, yellow, brown, like an old hippie poster, were playing mahjongg. And, oh my God, eating the *stobhach*!

A guy in a frayed, child-sized Mr. Natural T-shirt which barely reached his ribcage was dancing around Coo with a light meter. Someone had apparently taken Timmy's father's old four-string banjo down from the wall and bought it a beer. It perched on a bar stool in an old-timey tableau. One girl had a ferret.

"It's the Ikea Ferry, don't you see, Lass? The neighborhood's coming back, like Collins' men, and The Balus — the bar with it."

"You're gonna have to lose that borrowed brogue, then. Lad o' mine. That is, unless you wanna call the bar Paddy's."

His colorless, Saharan eyes darkened at the reference to Timmy, then brightened as he vaulted himself, sideways, over the bar. The stick.

"You're right, of course, God love ya, but t'won't be easy. For how am I to lose what I never had? Stout?"

"Okay. But cold."

"Ah, you were ever a philistine, wee Isabelle Oytsershifl."

"You're just twigging to that now?"

"No," he said, and put the beer before me. "Didn't I know it'all along? But Timmy loved you."

In the barback mirror, the one I fight, *my* eyes darkened. Not that it made much difference. I look like hell in every mirror. Purple black streaks under my eyes, the color of a ringworm infection; the rest of my face the ashy yellow you get when anemia robs the reds and browns out of dark-complected flesh. And I am stupid skinny. A hollow joke.

"Out with it . . . *then*," I said quietly, smiling with as much gentleness as I could muster.

Smiling, the muscles totally untutored. Smiling fucking *hurt*, and I felt my chapped bottom lip tear in the center. I sipped at the beer foam.

"You don't look well, Izzy," Mark said.

"No shit, Mark. But that's kind of an arcane name for a bar."

"What?"

"You don't look well, Izzy."

"I'm serious, Kid. You were lovely, you know. You know

what Timmy said? When he came in here after he met you?"

"Timmy came to the *bar* when he met me?"

"To check with Boris," we both said in unison.

"He said 'Mark, man. You ever wondered what Whitey Ford was up to all those years? I mean, what those curves balls were *about*? What I think is, I think he was trying to carve *this* girl out of the space in the battery.'"

And it is in this moment that the weight of my loneliness, a factor but not a fatal one all these months, finally crushes me. I look down because I cannot stand it, wait for the last bit of life's blood to drain out of me at last. But somehow, horribly, I keep breathing in and out.

I look up and Mark's eyes are wet. There is chaos behind us. The ferret has escaped, fled behind the jukebox which is playing "Dark Lady," its most modern selection. The noise and commotion is incredible, more action than this bucket of blood has seen in years.

"Everybody calm down," Mark bellows and everyone calms down.

"Good," he says. "Now let's keep it calm, and I'm sure the creature will come out on his own. When he does, I'll stand you all to a jar."

"The Leap," he says to me, without preamble.

"Mark. You can't."

"I already have," he says. "That young man is making the sign for me."

He gestures at the guy in the tiny Mr. Natural shirt.

"The boy with no shoes."

"He says they make his feet smell."

"I'm going home," I say.

Coo is at the door as I approach.

"I'm afraid of rats," he says.

"It's a ferret."

"What's the difference? Nasty things. Had a girl on the slab once, bit up by them. Going home to riff on Leap?"

"What do you think about it, Coo?"

"I think it's crass, but who listens to me? I'm just a sour old scratch bum, about to be run outta my bar by noisy kids with rats."

"A scratch bum with a million dollar South Brooklyn brownstone. Timmy started his troupe with fleas from the scratch bums in here."

"I remember it well. Mr. Chin and The General, we called 'em. Cheerful fellers they were, too, in spite of their circumstances. And they were happy to comply, so long as he bought 'em a shot for each bug."

"Some scratch bum you are, you don't even have fleas."

"A drunk's a drunk, Izzy. And a dead guy's still dead, no matter what you call his father's bar. Go home, Izzy. Riff on Leap. Make yourself crazy. Stare at the fleas. Build that pyre higher still."

"You go home too, Coo. Your wife's probably got dinner waiting."

"She does, you know. After all these years. Place settings. Candles. The whole she-bang. She'll sit there 'til 'leven or twelve, crying her eyes out, then wrap everything in foil, cover herself in cold cream and sleep the sleep of the righteous."

His voice is hard. But his eyes are wet. Good. Two for two. Who else can I hurt?

This isn't right. It is wrong in its essence. Unholy. I felt myself die in the bar, listening to Mark, to Timmy's words, felt my soul leave my body. Know the ferret fled because of it. I shouldn't be on the subway, sucking in air, reading ads for laser eye surgery.

But wait. I don't believe in my soul. So I guess it doesn't

matter. Riff on Leap, is that what he said? Go home and build my case against The Leap? And in favor of what? Paddy's? De Valera's Limp? One-Eyed Jack's? What do I care what he calls his bar?

But a leap, you know, is a lateral motion. Crossways, joyous, along the x-axis. A flea can leap 150 times its length laterally, along the x-axis. The two middle sections of its back legs stretch at once and it lets loose, head over heels overhead, landing on its feet, even if it is upside-down, because its middle legs turn up while its rear legs stretch back.

A flea's leap. Lateral. Along the x-axis. And to anyone, it is a thing of joy and beauty.

150 times its own length. That's *far*. If a man could do it, if Timmy could do it, leap, I mean, laterally, rather than plummet which anyone can do for any length, delimited only by an interposing surface like mud and concrete and alley cat shit which stops the fall and shatters the plummeter—if Timmy could leap 150 times his own length, well, let's see.

Six feet of long sweet Timmy flesh. 150 times that is 900. 900 feet. But what does that mean to a city kid like me? A block is one twentieth of a mile, or so they teach in Essex County elementary schools. And a mile is 5280 feet. So a block is a twentieth of 5280 feet. $(.05)(5280) = 264$. A block is 264 feet. How many blocks in a Timmy flea leap of 900 feet? $264x = 900$. $x = 900$ divided by 264. 3.409090, repeating. Repeating, as they taught us to say. In Watsessing Elementary on Locust Avenue in Bloomfield, New Jersey.

Almost three and a half blocks. Now wouldn't that be a spectacle? A joyous thing? Watching Timmy leap three and a half blocks? Conjuring the knots in his oatmeal-colored calves, as I used to knead them soft under my fingers, I almost think he could do it. And it would be beautiful, right? I mean, anyone would think so, to see a man of Timmy's stature leap that far, blond and happy, land on his big feet? Throw back his head and laugh?

But you see my problem with this, and thus the name for the bar. Timmy didn't leap, he jumped. Fell. Along the y-axis. Went kerplunk. Shattered.

And not 900 feet, but only fifty-two. I know because I measured the distance before I boarded up the back window with medium density fiberboard and sheetrock and muslin. I dug out Timmy's 100-foot Lufkin tape measure and fed the metal ribbon out the window. 'Til it hit where Timmy hit. Fifty-two feet.

Back then I was concerned with a different problem. Calculating Timmy's terminal velocity. Well, not exactly. I wanted to know how fast that son of a bitch fell. How long it took him to hit the ground in the airshaft and turn all my hopes and dreams to ash.

A body in motion, as I told the cops on the scene, accelerates at a rate of thirty-two point two feet per second per second. If we say that the body in question (though it was not yet a body then) had an initial position of fifty-two feet (the window) and a final position of zero feet (the bottom of the airshaft) at which point the body in motion ceased to be in motion, and became a body in earnest; and if we further conjecture no (or an immeasurably small) amount of initial velocity, and given minimal wind resistance in a tenement airshaft and such, if we also factor in only a tiny, negligible fraction of upness, as it were, then we can determine the speed of that transformation (from body in motion to body in earnest) with this little beauty of a formula:

$y = y0 + v0t + (½a)t^2$.

Y is for vertical position. T is for time. A is for acceleration. V is for velocity.

$y = y0 + v0t + (½a)t^2$.

$$0 = 52 + 0\frac{ft}{s}t + \frac{1}{2}(32.2\frac{ft}{s^2})t^2$$

Which would seem almost impossible to solve, except that mathematics gives us the quadratic key here, cloaked in a saucy little cocktail number I like to call

$$0 = ax^2 + bx + c$$

$$x = \frac{-b \pm \sqrt{b^2 - 4ac}}{2a}$$

Which means that

$$t = \frac{0 \pm \sqrt{0 \quad 4(16.1)(52)}}{2(16.1)} = \frac{\pm\sqrt{\quad 64.4(52)}}{32.2} = \frac{\pm\sqrt{3348.8}}{32.2} = \frac{\pm 57.8}{32.2} = 1.795$$

1.795 seconds or so. Ish.

Almost 1.8 seconds. To take Timmy's life from him, and mine from me. 1.8 seconds. Straight down into alley cat shit and concrete. I laugh out loud on the subway and the woman across from me automatically puts her arm around her sleeping son and pulls him closer. One-point-eight seconds straight down and splat. Who in his right mind would call that a leap? Who would commemorate such an act by rechristening a bar?

Unless. Unless we assume that Timmy's intention was to ascend, to jump rather than fall. That would be just like him, right? Maybe he figured that if he could jump as a flea jumps (only eighty times its length when we're talking about straight up, along the y-axis), the winds would simply cradle him, carry him ever upward.

And given six feet of Timmy, well now, wait a second. Six feet of Timmy. Eighty times that height is 480 feet. 264 feet in a block. If Timmy could jump as a flea jumps, straight up towards the heavens on naturally selected springs, he could jump 1.818, repeating, as they say in Watsessing Elementary, blocks.

1.8 blocks up. Or else 1.8 seconds to shatter. Mathematical sophistry? The coinkydink is purely narrative in nature? Well, so what? One-point-eight, I admit, is a terrible name for a bar. But it is certainly better than The Leap. I am a soulless monster on a lurching F train in the middle of the night. 1.8 is the best I can come up with under the circumstances.

Ain't math grand? 1.8. If I make myself very small, maybe I can curl up in the snowman's body of that point-eight.

And die.

13. Midnight Visitation

Mad ◆ Mangoes ◆ Massage of the Mons ◆ (Empress) Maud ◆ Maybe ◆ Meaning ◆ Medal ◆ Megafaunal Melodrama ◆ Mick ◆ Midnight Vistitation ◆ Million ◆ Mitigate ◆ More ◆ Mother ◆ Mourning

M is for Midnight Visitation. I am not privy to midnight visitation. I pray for it, but it does not come. True, I have no one to pray *to*, but I think the larger part of the problem is that I am simply not constitutionally suited to midnight visitation. I don't, for example, believe in ghosts.

Of course, it's also true that I've gone more or less batshit, which ought to mitigate my beliefs. If, when sane, you did not believe in ghosts, wouldn't it follow that once you were no longer sane, ghosts might exist? So you'd think (unless you paid any attention to logic sieves) but somehow, it just isn't so.

I am, in wishing for a midnight visitation, it seems to me, mad. Crazy, yes, okay. But why dwell on that? Mad crazy and also mad angry. Gypped. By any ordinary reckoning . . . oh, I know, nothing about you, Timmy—about *us* — was ordinary, but in the absence of you, you're not here.

And things are ordinary.

By any ordinary reckoning, you've bilked me out of my love and time and devotion. Years' worth. I gave them freely, I suppose, but I did not intend them to be free of meaning. Your absence strips my love and devotion of meaning. Your death makes the long hours I logged loving you seem stupid. I realize this complaint seems cocky, narcissistic . . . and pedestrian. If you were here, I know what you'd say, laughing with all the warmth of the sun.

"What do you want, Kid, a medal, or a chest to pin it on?"

But in the absence of you, you're not here. In the absence of you, who cares what you'd say? In the absence of you, who are you to talk? I feel cheated. Of the meaning of my love and time and devotion.

And how can I seek redress, Timmy? I mean, other than a midnight visitation in which I took some time out from licking your hands, drinking your salty, dizzying smell, clanging my teeth against yours to ball you out.

As *if*.

Well, okay. A medal. I want a medal. A monument to my lost time and love and devotion. A medal in lieu of meaning. Something tasteful, chipped from obsidian. Since that's not possible, and anyway, what would a girl *do* with something like that, I am mad.

Crazy with anger and fear and regret.

Mourning, I know, does not become me. Somebody stop me before I sink irrevocably into melodrama. Somebody kill me if I get moony. Somebody—anybody—kill me in any case. If I keep on like this, anything might happen. Who knows what will happen? I might start believing in astrology. I might start believing that the dead visit us in our dreams. I might spend all my time asleep, waiting for you to come to me.

My mother came to me in my dream last night. I fully realize that she was, in this guise, not at all an apparition. At most, she was a construct of my subconscious mind. In fact, I am rather more inclined to think of her as a product of random electrical impulses. For that matter, she was rather like a collection of random electrical impulses in life. That, or a burlap bag of snakes. But you get the idea. Pure chaos, in a skinny sausage casing.

In my dream she was very fat and blonde and happy as she

never was in life. (Not even blonde.) She said that the foreplay stinks in the afterlife but that she'd come to favor a kind of loose, left-handed massage of the mons. She said it in Yiddish. *Me ken brekhn*, she said. The foreplay makes you puke.

But, she said, resigned, smiling, *me ken mahkn dem kholem greser vi di nakht.*

One can make the dream bigger than the night.

"I'm leaving," I said in my sleep and woke up curled in pain like a larva naked on a spoon.

Make the dream bigger than the night. Whatever that means. Maybe one can, make the dream bigger than the night. Maybe *she* could. But for me the night is at critical mass. The night's so big, it encompasses the day. I am going into it, the night. Not gently. Gently's not my style. But not rage raging against it, either. Why rage rage, when you didn't, Timmy? I am going reasonably into the night.

Reason precludes astrology and seance, and midnight visitation. But not night, or stars. Some nights — nights are long when you're going into them — I try to stare up at the stars. But in a big smoky city, behind eyes that don't yet believe in astrology, this seems pointless. Some nights I take the ferry across the lower Hudson and sit on the Jersey-side, Jersey-style, with a domestic beer, and stare instead at the New York skyline.

The New York skyline is what greater metropolitan denizens have instead of stars, and I posit that the draw's the same; it's the same experience: the distance, the twinkling lights. Only the narrative is closer, the story more accessible. Eight million narratives, right? Still, that number's small, astronomically speaking. It's possible to connect the dots and come up with something less gnomic than twins or bears, dippers or archers or ball courts.

I'm not you, Timmy, just as you were not William Blake. I

don't have a visionary head. Visionary Heads don't come to me. If they did, I wouldn't be able to draw them, unless they were cobbled together from geometric solids.

I stare at the sky. I stare at the sky's line. I curl in pain like a naked larva. I dream of my Dead and write them ridiculous purple sex dialogue. But I'm not you, or Blake. Transcendence eludes me.

In 1819, having hooked up with the demented art teacher, séance-master and (gag) astrology buff John Varley, William Blake was visited by many an august personage. Ghosts of the famous dead swarmed before him to pose. Voltaire turned up. And Socrates. The Empress Maud. Richard the Lion-hearted. Colonel Blood. Herod, Caesar and Milton's first wife. King Saul of my people came twice, as his armor was too tricky to render in a single sitting. And Hotspur as he posed allowed as how he was bummed out to have been offed by Prince Henry, clearly an inferior assassin.

In this same phase, Blake was visited by the ghost of a flea. Like the others, the flea seized his chance to ham it up before the entranced artist. In fact the flea was so chatty, Blake had to leave off his first sketch and begin a second until his subject deigned to shut his trap, thus assuming his original pose.

And what did the flea report to William Blake, having been called across time and space for a midnight visitation? That fleas, "all fleas, are inhabited by the souls of such men as were by nature bloodthirsty to excess, and were therefore providentially confined to the size and form of insects; otherwise, were he himself for instance the size of a horse, he would depopulate a great portion of the country."

By way of bragging coda, he also opined that he, and by extension all fleas, could swim.

Timmy, of course, did not care for this chapter in Flea

Literary History. For one thing, he didn't believe fleas were evil. Beyond that, though he didn't think fleas were evil, and didn't, for that matter, believe in reincarnation, he couldn't get with the way modern art historians, with their predilection for post-mortem psychoanalysis, approach that period of Blake's work with the zeal of professional debunkers. As if, in attempting a critical analysis of the Visionary Heads, their primary task was to prove that Blake was *not*, in fact, visited by ghosts.

I suppose that it's true that whether Blake was actually visited by ghosts, or merely believed himself to be visited by ghosts, has no bearing on the work itself. And is certainly nobody's business. Inspiration, as Timmy used to say, is its own thing.

My concern here is more with the fact that certain people, like Blake and like Timmy, are open to inspiration. And to believing they might be visited by ghosts; and thus are open to being so visited. Round about midnight. As they shiver in their beds, sipping cocoa, or swapping religious lies with gregarious astrologists.

These are people, like Blake and like Timmy, for whom change, real change, is not only possible but necessary. They are a whole sub-species and are capable of tectonic change. Biblical change. Epochal change. Change on an evolutionary scale.

Me? I am not of that order. Or rather, I am. I am of that kingdom. I am of that phylum. I am of that class. I am of that order. I am of that family, that genus, even that species. But I am not that kind of animal.

During the Pleistocene era, when eighteen-foot sloths, and beavers the size of steroidal bears and armadillos who looked like VW bugs were the norm, the local plants, taking in the size and scope of the dominant fauna, adjusted themselves accordingly. Leastways the evolutionary pressures which made megafauna a good bet swept the plants along in their wake.

Thus we have avocados and gingkos, honey locusts and osage oranges; mangoes, Kentucky coffee trees and the preternaturally stinky durian. All these are fruits who've designed themselves for partnership with giant animals, animals who could swallow their toxic or giant seeds whole, excrete them whole, disperse them.

These are some big critters, no kidding. We don't see anything like 'em except here and there in Southern Africa and tropical Asia. The last of the North American megafauna checked out 13,000 years ago.

13,000 years seems long to me, because a day seems long to me. A day without Timmy's seal-bark laugh. But 13,000 years isn't long enough for the plants partnered up with these sumo-herbivores to notice that they're flying solo, to make the necessary adjustments for survival in a new age.

Those few that have survived have done so only in a diminished state, or because people took a liking to their flesh and took to planting the seeds on purpose, for their own ends. Animals, like us (and like bugs), which eat fruits without doing anything useful about dispersing their seeds, maintaining their variety, are called pulp thieves.

Maybe I am not open to midnight visitation because I am like a widowed megafaunal plant. Some time has passed, true. Almost seven months and that's *long*. But not enough time for me to notice, on a cellular level, that my evolutionary partner is gone for good.

And if this is true, doesn't it follow that it's the pulp thieves who are keeping me going? People and bugs who have taken a liking to my flesh, who nourish me along, week after week, fattening my soul for the slaughter?

I should be grateful to them, I guess. But I can't be. I blame them for keeping me going. I blame them for keeping me safe from midnight visitation. Ghosts don't come if you don't believe in them. And ghosts don't come back if you don't believe they're gone in the first place.

How do you tell a widowed megafaunal plant when you see one? It has a fibrous pulp, or a tough rind, or a big pit, or a long stiff pod, or it stinks to high heaven. Or else it stares through the night on the banks of the lower Hudson, in frayed jeans and an old Dirt Club T-shirt, reserving its seeds for some big lummox of a mick who'll never come again.

Named ◆ Naturally ◆ Naphtali ◆ Narrowback ◆ Naught ◆ Negates
Neophyte ◆ New Jersey ◆ Newel ◆ Nihility ◆ No ◆ Non-stop Fun ◆ Nothing
Nourishment ◆ Nullity ◆ Null set ◆ Numb ◆ Numbers ◆ Nuzzling (my neck)

N is for Narrowback. Narrowback was Timmy's nickname from his father, was what a lot of Irish immigrants called their first-generation American sons. Narrowback, that is to say, they didn't have to haul themselves through life on the strength of their shoulders, weren't, you know, working stiffs.

Technically, I think, Timmy wasn't a narrowback. He worked on ships to put himself through school and was broad astem as a result, even if he was narrow through the stern, lean and supple, with long, fibrous muscles like a yogi.

But never mind. The fact remains that Timmy's father called him, Timmy, Narrowback; and didn't call Mark, who never left his side, Narrowback.

Narrowback. There is dismissal in that word, of course. But also some sneaky pride. Dismissal and pride, a potent combination, leading, I guess inexorably, to exile.

But I suppose it's a tricky bit of business, a father's love. People are always trying, trying and failing, to earn it. Well, naturally. Otherwise, why would they always be yearning for their Gods? Abandonment. Conditional love. Exile. What a tedious mess it all is.

I say I suppose, because my own father's abandonment was total. And unconditional. I do not have to wonder what I did to lose it. He lit out before my mother was even, as they said back then, showing. An unusual thing for a Jewish man to do, with a community to answer to. But he didn't stick around for their scorn. And I expect he had his reasons.

Of their brief marriage, my mother had only one thing to say, but she was fond of saying it.

"*Es geven shlept vi goles,*" it dragged itself out like the exile.

By "the exile," she meant of course *The* Exile. The big one. The one started by the Romans' squashing vise around 70 anno domini (*year of* your *Lord, maybe, but these are not my people.*) the big-heap wandering homelessness for which my people are legend. Abandoned. Unprotected. Yearning. For century after century. Attempting to live by a fantastically complex set of rules which, as they spread out into the big bad world, and time spread with them, began to make less and less sense. Rules which were not necessarily the best tools for navigating the brief, angry arc of an entire human life, especially alone, abandoned, unprotected. And for what? The promise of a safe home, protection, a Father's love?

That my mother described her six-month marriage to my father in these terms always puzzled me. But, as I say, I didn't know the guy. And his abandonment of me was unconditional. Having never known my father's love, I do not have to worry about how I failed to keep it.

I do, however, worry about how I failed to keep your love, Timmy. I wonder why I am in exile. Oh, I know that makes no sense, isn't healthy, or even rational, but that's the way it feels.

You were so fun, Timmy, so easy and open and calm, so full of life, a startling lickable hunk of grace. A grace popsicle. Grace on a stick. Quiescently frozen grace confection, fused to a tongue depressor. Living every moment, occupying your every cell with *presence.*

To me, it seemed a religion.

And I was a neophyte, a convert to the non-stop fun. The conversion came hard, you know. I was a serious kid before I fell in with you. A math geek, working in a bank. Patterns of numbers criss-crossed my head, a dangerous structure of tangled bird's-mouth ladders. Fun wasn't among my experiences, and it wasn't among my goals.

When I fell, I fell hard. Into grace. Into grace rather than from it, but the trajectory's the same. The path a moving me follows through space as a function of time: Straight down and splat.

So here I am, a convert, still a neophyte, and the beguiling son-of-a-bitch who turned me out has, in no uncertain terms, abandoned the faith. Abandoned me to a faith which, without Timmy as pimp, seems impossible. Non-stop fun? What does that even mean? And why adhere to a fantastically complex set of rules which no longer makes any sense?

Meanwhile, the shrinks and radio pundits and barflies keep telling me I'm supposed to find a way to live. Now, what way would that be, do you think? Non-stop fun? Not hardly. There has been a serious stoppage in the fun. Or back to the numbers, the serious ambitious tangle of patterns. Cold, clean, crisp. But how can I? When in the meantime, I've known joy?

Well, you can see how my thoughts might turn to abandonment, to exile, to fathers and their curious belief systems, but what profit is there in such an inquiry? I shove the thoughts back down into my consecrated throat and try to keep plodding along. I stick one tentative paw back into the crisp tangle of numbers in my head and find that the dangerous structure has begun to collapse. It is shot through with a longing its straight lines cannot accommodate. Its newel wobbles, made of the jelly, the pigshod jelly, you've made of me.

N is for Numbers, for nothing, for the nullity they bring.

225 days since Timmy died.

1977, the year of my birth.

238-3289, the phone number of Stubby's Transmissions in Englishtown, New Jersey—my all time number one favorite road sign.

1683, the year the first bar in Jersey—or, as we said back then, the Jerseys—opened its doors.

And 38,077 which was the population of Bloomfield, New Jersey in 1930, the putative birth year of my putative father, putative son of the house of Naphtali.

N is for numbers and also for numb. These words are almost the same to me. They sure sound the same, and I use one to achieve the other. But numb and numbers are not, in fact, related. The English word numb is old as the hills, old beyond reckoning. It first appears in the Middle English, *nimmen*, to take. Numbers came to English through a different route, the fifteenth century Latin *numerus*, a sum of units.

Of course the *idea* of numb is as old as the feelings it negates. And numbers? Well, I can only presume there have been numbers at least as long as there have been things to count. A fuck of a long time. Longer ago even than the conscription, by God, through Moses, of the putative house of my putative father.

Naphtali. 53,400 men over twenty years of age in the tribe. Or so it says in Numbers, the fourth book of Moses. Among them, my father's ancestor. Well, what difference does it make? I am sure that, unlike me, he did not seem putative to himself. At least he was counted, right? Named by his God.

N is for numbers, for null set, for nihility.

30, 31, 32, 33, 34, the ages most eminent mathematicians

peaked creatively. Entomologists, according to the psychometrists who study such things, have a slightly wider spread: 30 31 32 33 34 35 36 37 38 39.

Psychometrists are partial to a test called "Memory Span for Digits Forward and Memory Span for Digits Backward," quite a mouthful, to be sure. But the title is descriptive. Ninety percent of the adult population can easily repeat between five and eight digits which have been read to them. That same ninety percent can repeat between four and six digits in reverse order.

Try it yourself, on your kid or your neighbor or your dog. Try it with these numbers:

8-6-0

1-5-3-8

2-5-2-6-8

7-4-9-0-9-5

2-4-2-1-3-8-9

0-1-8-5-1-5-0-9

6-7-5-6-7-0-3-9-1

4-0-1-8-7-3-9-7-2-0

Now try it backwards.

5-1-4

4-9-5-7

0-5-6-9-2

3-7-4-8-6-1

8-5-2-6-4-3-7

Curiously, my own ability to repeat digits backward is wildly high. Off the charts. The tester invariably runs out of digit sequences or patience before I ever falter.

Numbers. Aren't they ridiculous? Whatever made me think I could draw nourishment from them like a plant turned to the sun? I turn, but the light's not there. N is for numbers, the fourteenth stage of grief. Among them, I am alone in a pith helmet.

Everything you said and did, Timmy, it seems to me, was true. I mean both, of course. That you never lied to me, and also true in the carpenter's sense, or the cartographer's. But the true fact that you killed yourself negates those earlier truths, which of course makes me want to leap to the conclusion that you didn't really kill yourself.

Leap? Right, well, let's leave that alone for the moment. Here I am less concerned with my own suicide ideation, because, I mean, *duh*, than I am with analyzing my stupid paradox in terms of classic logic games.

Suppose instead of nuzzling my neck, showing me fleas, stealing Altamont, you had seduced me with the following proposition: will you promise to live a life full of joy and adventure with me if I make a true statement and to let me kill myself if I make a false statement? And suppose I said okay, I'll bite. And then you said you won't live a life full of joy and adventure with me and you won't let me kill myself.

If I then proceeded to live a life full of joy and adventure with you, your statement would be false, in which case, I'd have broken my promise. Which would pretty much cut me out of any chance of living a life of joy and adventure with you, if I didn't want to be a sleazy, lying, promise-breaking son-of-a-bitch. But if I also didn't let you leap out of our window, your statement would become true, in which case, to keep my promise, I'd have to live a life full of joy and adventure with you which I couldn't do and still keep my promise, because then your statement would be false.

The set-up, you see, is rigged. I never had a shot at living a life full of joy and adventure with you. If I am to honor my promise, I have to let you kill yourself. Assuming I am honorable, I am powerless to prevent your suicide.

And destined to live a life without you. Or joy. Or adventure.

And that's how it turned out, right? But Timmy, you never gave me that choice. You never gave me a chance to say "no, I will not promise to live a life full of joy and adventure with you if you make a true statement and to let you kill yourself if you make a false statement." If you had, I don't think I'd have gone for it. I'd have known, I think, intuitively, that your suicide wasn't up to me. I'd have seen it for what it was.

A raw deal.

I say I don't *think* I'd have gone for it because I'm not now the girl I was then. And I can only make subjective guesses about her also subjective motivations. I don't really know what I would have done before. Not now.

Now I'm a neophyte, yearning for non-stop fun. I'm a wandering Jew. A creature of reason whom reason has abandoned. A soldier of logic, gored by the indeterminate. I'm alone in a pith helmet, newly made mewling, bereft except for the numbers.

N is for numbers.

$Y(t)$ = height above ground at time t.

$Y0$ = height above ground at time 0 (52').

$V(t)$ = Velocity at time t.

$V0$ = initial vertical velocity (positive means up, negative means down, we assume 0.)

g = acceleration due to Earth's gravity (-32.2 ft/s/s, down is negative in this example.)

Y at time 0 sec = 52 - 16.1 x 0 x 0 = 52 - 0 = 52 feet.

Y at time 1 sec = 52 - 16.1 x 1 x 1 = 52 - 16.1 = 35.9 feet. (The Cat Lady's apartment. Seems about right.)

Y at time 2 sec = 52 - 16.1 x 2 x 2 = 52 - 64.4 = -12.4 feet (Already hit the ground.)

Nineteen choruses of "I'm no good for you, Baby," sung by my pre-Timmy beau. Forty strokes per minute when we caress our lovers' long monkey arms. 14,218 1971 Plymouth

Road Runners sold. 253 kinds of fleas known to exist in North America. Seventeen times I've turned the radio off and on again since nightfall. 972 strikeouts pitched by Sid Fernandez for the New York Mets between 1984 and 1989. $6.99 for 24, the price of condoms at the Good Luck Pharmacy on Grand Street.

Forty miles per hour, a force eight gale on the Beaufort scale, the speed of my sneeze as repressed tears swell the embattled flesh around my eyes. $2^{3,021,377} - 1$, one of the largest known prime numbers, a 909,526-digit whopper. 3,021,377 is itself a prime number; for comparison, it has, obviously, like the annual salary of my ultra-boss at the bank, only seven digits. But both are prime numbers, divisible, like 2, 3, 5, 7, 11 and me, only by ourselves and one.

Two pudding women on the subway. Three times in rapid succession a man shouted "muthafucka look older than Methuselah" on Howard Street as I came down the block. Five dead mice Altamont has stored in my cowboy boot. Seven layers of cremated Timmy-skin in an urn in Brooklyn. Eleven offers of pre-approved credit cards Timmy has received since he died. Thirteen times I've been stupid and cruel.

Think I'm topped out there? Just watch me now.

N is for naught.

Object ◆ Occupy ◆ Off ◆ Oh ◆ (engine) Oil ◆ Okay ◆ Old ◆ Open ◆ Oppressive ◆ Optimistic ◆ Option Orderly ◆ Ordinary ◆ Oscillating ◆ Ossuaries ◆ Ourselves ◆ Out ◆ Over ◆ Oytsershifl (treasure ship)

O is for Over. I am, they keep telling me, supposed to get over it. Get over you, Timmy. Move on. Find a way to live. Turn the other cheek. Get over you. Start sleeping with someone new. Immerse myself in a project. Don't get too tired or hungry, angry or lonely. Help the elderly. Volunteer as an orderly. Work with disabled children. Give blood.

Out with the old. In with the new. The king is dead; long live the king. Get over it.

But I don't seem to be getting over it. If anything, if this doesn't seem too trite, it appears to have gotten over me. Squatted down right on top of me, sealed off any exit. We bury the dead and they reside under us. We build on the dead, live over them.

That's what we tell ourselves, right? We like to think of death that way. Castles built on ossuaries. But on any street, you can see people like me, slumped under a tremendous weight, empty-eyed, and it is clear that they are not over it. They are not living and building, on top of the foundation of the past. They are not even living.

They are not over the dead; they are under them.

Timmy is dead but his oppressive weight resides over me. I cart it around all day, 'til the day is over. And at night, freed from the bonds of my non-belief, it makes itself even heavier.

O is for over. I turn over in bed, awakened by Timmy's behemoth weight shifting over me, and touch Pudge Goroguchi's strange body. Strange body? Well, no. His body is lovely, strong and classically proportioned, scarred just enough to make it his own. It is strange only because it's a body next to me. A body. An embodiment of his only sin as far as I know.

One sin. But it's a doozy.

He is guilty of not being Timmy.

"Oytsershifl," he mutters. "What does it mean?"

"It means treasure ship."

"Treasure ship? Like a pirate?"

"Yeah, Pudge. Like a pirate."

He laughs in his sleep. This boy is so good-humored he even laughs in his sleep.

"Dangerous pirate girl," he murmurs, "crazy sad pirate girl, *kichigai sanishii kaizokou onna*," he murmurs. "No wonder you're so hard to satisfy."

"Hey," I say, and elbow him. "I get off pretty easy compared to some girls."

"You get *off* easy, Iz. But then you want a transfer."

He laughs himself back into sleep.

I have been, it is true, insatiable. But because Pudge is so good-natured, and because in fucking the widow of his intellectual hero, he is himself engaged in some kind of mourning ritual, and because sometimes, when I am fucking him, I disappear from myself, and because it is an open secret between us that he is not Timmy, I think this bears no special scrutiny. Let him think I always was this way. What difference does it make?

I skirt along the barest edge of sleep, wake choking under Timmy's heft. Airshaft has wedged himself between me and my sleepover guest. He stares at me levelly. I reach to pet him but my hand keeps reaching, over the now blinking cat, to touch the

122

strange body next to mine. Not strange. But, you know. Strange.

"What does Goroguchi mean?"

"The mouth of the fifth son."

"Oh," I say.

Oh. O is for Oh which we say when we don't know what to say—when we don't know what to say, and saying something we *do* know, like the fact that, when represented in decimal form, a rational number always terminates or resolves in a repeating pattern, isn't an option.

Like any good rational number, I could terminate, but I haven't. Yet. Or else I could resolve in a repeating pattern, which I guess I'm still doing. Ten years with Timmy out of a grand total of thirty-four lived so far. If you could call it grand. If you could call it living.

Either way, it's a rational number. Five-seventeenths. Five-seventeenths of my life. .2941176470588235, repeating, as they taught us to say in Watsessing Elementary.

A rational number, when represented as a decimal, always terminates, or else resolves itself in an endlessly repeating pattern. For something to say which you do know, when you don't know what to say, it's a mouthful, right? Over-packed with emotion. I guess that's why O is for oh, an exclamation, a word stand-in for all our emotions.

And calculations.

Oh.

Oh, as in, he lived unknown and few could know/ when Timmy ceased to be/ but he is in his grave, and oh,/ the difference to me.

To Pudge, of course, Timmy was quite known, which is why I'm still sleeping with him—with *him*, and, yes, with him. With him, Tim. Just so we're clear, my motivations, sick though they might be, are not obscure to me. I may be crazy, maybe even probably am. But I am not stupid. I am not deluding myself.

The charred shards had a certain tragic panache, I'll admit—*Ben Wa* Timmy! But I couldn't keep that up forever. Mark might miss them, sooner or later, the shards I mean. And besides, a girl needs a little friction. Friction, resistance.

Something to kick against, buck against. Something to interpose between myself and inertia, because an object in motion, even if that motion is a downward spiral, will tend to remain in motion. Unless acted upon by an outside force. Thus friction, resistance. Bucking.

Friction? Bucking? It sounds so crass. And inertia, resistance, the implication of movement? It sounds so hopeful. But I don't mean it like that. I don't intend either. Hopeful or crass. I only mean that I'm not fooling myself.

And, thank heaven for small favors ('cause that's the only kind we get), I am not fooling Pudge Goroguchi either. Straight from the mouth of the fifth son, he swears he knows what he's getting himself into. Whether he can handle it once he gets there, well, he can manhandle that hulking *Oytsershifl* of a muscle car as if it's a shred of stripper's Lycra panties, I guess he can handle anything. I'm unlikely to be around for the fallout at this rate, so what difference does it make?

Night turns into morning, when he has to move his beautiful car, or risk it towed, or battered by Chinatown trucks of tofu and knock-off perfume. Wholesale vegetables. Fake watches and handbags. Flat-billed baseball caps, sorted by gang color rather than team. Why would someone drive a car like that, through commuter and commercial traffic, to New York City? *How* would someone drive a car like that through commuter and commercial traffic to New York City?

Night turns into morning in a blur of alcohol, cat scratches, exchanged murmurs. Dream flashes of Timmy combing though my tangled brown hair with his foot like a monkey. Night turns into mourning, another morning, and how stale all this is getting. Am I really supposed to get up out of this rumpled bed and live through another entire day? Occupy this aching shell for twenty-four more hours?

"I have time to do the fleas for you, if you want," he says.

I shrug. Not petulant. I really don't care. Except that I don't want any favors. But he likes tending to them, so what's the difference? One less empty gesture to make today. One less empty gesture more or less.

He laughs. A shrug can make this boy laugh.

"Why the long face, Sunshine?"

He laughs. He cracks himself up, this guy. Even I smile. What a question.

"Does your name have a story?" he asks, setting the artificial dog whirring, collecting the newly-hatched fleas in his palm, poking them, doting on them.

"Not really. My great-grandfather made it up at Ellis Island. I guess he was feeling optimistic. Does yours?"

"Well, probably, right? But I don't know it. My father came to Iowa State for a Chemistry Master's. He fell in love with a farmer's daughter, moved back to Kansas with her, took a plough to the back forty. He doesn't like to talk about his family in Japan. Bad farmers, is all he'll say. But I'm guessing some ancestor made my name up too."

"In the Meiji restoration?"

"So you know about that," he says, as if it's a state secret—no, as if the fact that your ordinary, run of the mill, non-noble Japanese only got surnames in the 1860s was something he was explicitly trying to keep from me.

"I know a little bit about everything, Kansas. That's the thing about me."

"Oh, *that's* the thing about you? 'Cause I was wonderin'."

I don't like it.

It's too easy, flirty, intimate. What if he starts feeling something and I have to be responsible for his great big stupid heart? Or worse, what if I do?

"Does this seem like a good idea to you?"

He ambles to the bed, hands outstretched, but full of larvae.

"What? Sleeping with you? Our torrid little claustrophobic affair? Driving a 65,000 dollar car to Chinatown? Fucking a man's wife in full view of his fleas? What, specifically?"

I sigh.

"Any of it."

I look at the larvae. They're wriggling and white, some as big as five millimeters, some as small as half a millimeter. One half. Point five. A rational number, but still grotesque. In wriggling they repeat. In excreting iron, hardening their cuticles, they turn into fleas. Terminate. Terminate, or at least move on to the next thing. Get over it.

"When you saw Timmy perform, did he do the Bertolotto tribute?"

Unlike Mark and me, when you mention Timmy to Doctor of Parasitology Edward "Pudge" Goroguchi, his eyes light up.

He drops the larvae on the bed, gestures expansively, rubs his hands together like a greedy fly.

"The second time," he says. "No, the third. It was cool. He had adult *pulex irritans*, dozens of them, all dressed in top and tails like Bertolotto, and he had them enact a passage from Bertolotto's book while he read it to theremin music. Can you imagine? Adult fleas. In top hats, moving in a circle, playing larval fleas."

The larvae are oscillating. No, they're squirming. Across the sheets, toward me and Airshaft. I look at them, at Pudge. He scoops them up again.

"Yeah," I say, "I saw the routine. What I mean is, do you remember the passage?"

"How could I forget it? It's the epigraph in his thesis."

He goes back to the tank, flicks all the larvae but two into their appropriate chambers. His intonation is lilting, sing-song, like him, almost Japanese.

"'It is worthy of remark,' he chants, 'that if two of these little worms are enclosed in a narrow space, deprived of food, they will attack each other, and each taking hold with its mouth of its adversary's tail, so as to form a ring, will eat one another. This ring becoming smaller and smaller every day for five or six successive days, without either of them leaving their hold, until they finally die, and becoming dry, are sufficiently hard to be preserved.'"

He takes my left hand and wraps the two maggots around the ring finger, laughing.

"What's your point, Izzy? That we're eating each other? That we're becoming smaller? That we're worms? That you want a ring?"

Now I laugh. Hollowly. Bitterly.

"Yeah, Pudge. That last one. That must be my point. That I want a ring."

He sighs, takes my hand in his, squishing the larvae between my fingers.

"I'm just an entomologist," he says.

"I know."

"A guy entomologist."

"I know."

"Yeah, you know a little about everything, Jersey. That's the thing about you."

He laughs, starts dressing. Watching him dress, it occurs to me that we are both naked. Naked as little white worms. Worse.

Naked. And touching worms.

"I'm an entomologist. I'm a guy. You've got bugs and the sex is good. I don't care how fucked up the situation is."

"And the ride?"

"My car? My car is my car. Formidable and vulnerable, which happens to be how I like 'em."

"Cars?"

"Yeah, Iz. Cars."

"Okay, then."

"Okay?"

"Yeah, okay."

Okay.

Okay. Formidable and vulnerable? Right well, okay. But if I'm supposed to destroy this guy, take him down, I want a piece of his car too. I don't have a taste for blood.

Not blood. And not lymph, choler, bile or phlegm either. Bodies and their constituent parts, who cares? Really. Only my own demise interests me.

But brake fluid? Engine oil? Antifreeze? High-Octane gasoline? The four bodily humours of the classic American performance vehicle?

I don't have a taste for blood.

But car juice? Now, that's another story.

16. PERFECT

Parasite ◆ Pascal ◆ Past ◆ Perfect ◆ Perforce ◆ Periodic (table of elements)
Pets ◆ Pit ◆ Plankton ◆ Point ◆ Pounced ◆ Pray ◆ Pregnant ◆ Preposterous
Primary Task ◆ Prodigy ◆ Properties ◆ Protozoa ◆ Provide ◆ Pythagoras

P is for Perfect. I did not, before I hooked up with Timmy, have any particular notion about what characteristics went into the perfect partner. I was a creature of reason, not given to flights of fancy, lottery tickets or zodiac charts; not given to gambling on preposterous odds.

But it is not simply a matter of not believing in a perfect soul mate in the first place. Nor is it a matter of my having believed that a perfect soul mate for me existed, but, given the billions of people I'd have to sort through to get there, not believing I'd have much chance of running into him.

I simply never gave the matter any thought at all. Things that did not yield to reason, like God or lottery tickets or absinthe-voiced entomologists, didn't interest me. Perfection, true love, homeopathy—they simply don't make good house pets for creatures of reason.

Perfect means "past" to a linguist, and "finished" to a purist. To a pissant math prodigy, perfect means something else altogether. Perfect comes to us rationalists from the decidedly irrational Pythagoras and means a number that equals the sum of all the numbers which divide evenly into it. Six is divisible by one, two and three. One plus two plus three equals six. Twenty-eight is divisible by one, two, four, seven and fourteen. Add 'em up?

Twenty-eight.

That I should have been looking for a guy who was the sum of all the components which divided equally into him is, obviously, ridiculous. Had anyone (even Pythagoras, who was given to such nonsense) suggested that my primary task was to find a perfect man, I probably would have rolled my eyes.

Nevertheless, when the perfect man presented himself, I pounced. Pounced, giving it no thought. Pounced, as if I'd been programmed to do so. Mathematicians and scientists, rationalists who abandon the faith (reason) and take up Faith, such as one has in a God, or in true love, are said to be following a hot tip from Pascal. This is not a compliment.

Pascal gave up science and math at the age of thirty-two. His advice, and I suppose it made sense to him, was "do not hesitate to wager that God exists. If you win, you win everything." Of course, when the moment comes, and you abandon the sweet bounds of cold, clean reason, for love, or, I guess, for God, it doesn't feel like a decision or a wager. It feels like falling down a well.

You are simply in it. And a rational person, finding herself in an irrational situation, if she cannot backtrack, scrabble up the slick dank walls back to the relative sanctity of simple science, will probably figure she may as well enjoy the ride. And maybe take notes.

Anyhow, having known a perfect man, I now know what a perfect man is. He is capable and competent. Funny, and his good cheer fills the room. He comes to you in joy. He is good at what he does and digs doing it. He expects the same of you, meets you with equal force. Kids and animals are drawn to him. He has a beautiful sense of the absurd. Each new day is a curiosity to him. He clasps your body to his in the night. He is all these things.

And he is alive.

Whether a perfect man is like a perfect number, I'm not

sure. Whether a perfect man is, exactly, a sum of all those characteristics—whether those characteristics are equally divisible in him, I'm not sure.

Why am I not sure?

Because Timmies do not yield to reason. Timmies do not yield to mathematical autopsies. I wish they did. I'd flay that sucker on the slab, take samples, measure, bag, bottle, weigh and sterilize. Codify for all to see. I wish they did.

But they don't.

A perfect man may or may not embody the same characteristics as a perfect number. There's no way to know. But a perfect man is definitely alive. If he dies, in battle or on a dance floor or of injuries in an airshaft, he ceases to be perfect.

Like Blaise Pascal, when the moment came, I did not hesitate to abandon my faith in reason. If you win, you win everything.

But if you lose, well, what? When Pascal died, not only did he give up any shot he had at being someone's perfect man, but more importantly, his consciousness ceased. He never knew he lost his bet. Which brings us back to me. In the goddamn well.

I abandoned reason, but that's okay because reason, it would appear, is not a jealous God. When you abandon reason, it does not abandon you. Reason is always there. It cares not for your craziness. But if your abandonment of reason leads you to an irrational place, then reason perforce cannot release you.

I gave up so much to be with Timmy. Nothing tangible, you understand. He was not, as they say, a user. He gave as good as he got, always, in everything, and he expected the same of me. But I gave up my lack of belief that something as wonderfully crazy as Timmy could happen.

And when it was happening, and I was falling down a well, I could thrill to every minute of it. And I could pretend that I was still a creature of reason because I could make observations about the experience, about my happiness, about his, and tell myself that I was still doing good science. Sometimes good science is just observation. You don't have to know the explanation to be a creature of reason. You just have to believe that an explanation exists.

But I think I must've been kidding myself. Because when Timmy killed himself, he left me not only without him, the auburn hair on his wrists, the smell of chives and sweat; he left me in a world where an explanation doesn't exist. I'm lost. I'm lost because I don't know how to get around.

No explanations? Well, what else is there? What's here for me now? I don't know about magic or fate, ecstatic visions or mysterious suicides. I don't know about rage and sorrow. I know about rocks and numbers, plants and animals, the periodic table of elements.

I have tried to free myself. Free myself, right myself, find myself. Get oriented to this strange new world. The one without explanations—and without Timmy. In my own weird way, I really have.

I think of Pascal, of what he might have done if somehow he could have been conscious of the fact that he wagered wrong, if someone had been able to prove to him that God didn't exist, short of killing him, at which point, yes, he would've not gone to heaven, not won everything, but he wouldn't have known it. Because he was dead.

I suppose Pascal would have picked himself up, dusted himself off, returned himself to reason—which never abandons you, not even when you abandon it. But before he took on the next big question in seventeenth century physics, he would surely have tried to use reason, which always exists, to figure out where he went wrong, how he could have believed in God, who doesn't exist.

And reason cannot answer that question, because it exists outside of reason. It's a puzzler, right? A real head-scratcher? Which brings us back to me.

In the goddamn well.

I suppose I could pray for release. But to whom would I pray? Reason? God? The intercession of Timmy? No, I will have to engineer my own release, on my own terms. I don't think people are gonna like it. But who asked them?

Meanwhile, I am gathering information about how best to go about it. I mean, very well, I find myself at the bottom of this well. Timmy has abandoned me here but so far, reason has not. Reason doesn't work too well at the bottom of a well you fell into when you abandoned reason, but it is all I've got. What are the properties of this pit? How deep and wide is it? How dark? How dank? How cold? And where did I put my instruments?

I have an impulse to release all of Timmy's fleas into the apartment. Just kick the three smoked-glass tanks over and see what happens. I am resisting it, because I fear the fleas would kill Airshaft, just suck him dry. I would've stopped caring for them weeks ago—hell, I stopped caring for *myself*, and not caring for parasites is way easier than that—but somehow I don't.

At the very least, I'd like to stop using the Artificial Dog to breed more fleas, but Pudge keeps tending to it, and I haven't the will to tell him not to bother. Explaining is too hard. He invented the damn thing. So I keep feeding the fleas blood. Blood from bags and blood from live mice. Airshaft helps by dispatching the mice to the great mouse beyond once they are drained. And I keep feeding the human fleas on my body, letting Pudge watch as once Timmy did.

But in truth, caring for parasites is a drag. P is for Parasites, and caring for them is a motherfucking drag.

Parasites are not well-liked. This is common knowledge. Every living thing is supposed to pay its own way. Things that don't, malpractice lawyers and ticks, junkie boyfriends, tapeworms, elderly relatives, barnacles, protozoa, and, of course, fleas—they make us uncomfortable.

We make some exception for the symbiotes. The bacteria in our own intestines, which have made themselves essential to our digestion. Pregnancy, which provides us with an opportunity to reproduce our genetic material. But, though we can see the point of a symbiotic parasitical relationship, these too make us uncomfortable.

Although nature provides us with so many counter-examples as to reduce the idea to absurdity, we continue, *au fond*, to believe that every living creature ought to pay its own way. Parasites give us the creeps.

Why that should be, I'm not sure. Nor am I sure whether those same living creatures, once they are dead, are still expected to pay their own way. Parasites gives us the creeps. And the Dead give us the creeps. But I don't know if it's for the same reason.

The two main guys I've been with as an adult, one of them, granted, just an extension of the other. But still. The two main guys I've been with as an adult have been, by vocation, lovers of parasites. I don't mean to suggest that in loving me, or, anyway, in having me, they loved a parasite. Not me, man. Uh-uh. I've thought about it. And I'm sure. I've paid my own way, every step of that way.

But they are men who adore parasites. Which is weird, right? Crazy. *Mishuge*, as my mother said. Well, maybe not. Parasites are creatures who devise fantastically complex strategies for staying alive. They are devious survivors.

The European rabbit flea (*Spilopsyllus cuniculi Dale*) confines itself, absolutely, to the European rabbit. For that matter, it confines itself, almost exclusively, to the rabbit's thin-skinned, bloodful ears. Why? Because over the course of their extensive relationship, the rabbit flea has bound its own breeding cycle with that of the rabbit. A female rabbit flea cannot herself ovulate until she has fed on the blood of a pregnant European rabbit. And a male rabbit flea is indifferent to a female rabbit flea until she has fed on the blood of a newborn rabbit.

This would seem preposterously complex and unnecessary as a way to get by, except that the larvae of a European rabbit flea employing such a strategy necessarily have rabbit dung to live on and new rabbits-condos to move into right at hand. Or, I guess, foot. Perfect, right?

Parasites are devious survivors. Preposterous. Comical. Creepy. There is, in the South Seas, a crustacean whose primary task in life is to find a particular fish. Once it locates the fish of its dreams, the crustacean eats the fish's tongue and then replaces it. Replaces it. Wires itself right into the fish's mouth and draw its nourishment directly from the fish, like a real tongue. For its part, the fish too adapts. It can flex the crustacean, lick with it, scoop plankton with it. The crustacean replaces the actual tongue, and the two creatures continue on their way.

Parasites are devious survivors. Men who adore them are strange. Parasites are perfect survivors.

But I am not a survivor at all.

17. QUICKSILVER

Qiana ◆ Quack ◆ Quarry ◆ Quell ◆ Question ◆ Qui vive ◆ Quickened ◆ Quicksand
Quicksilver ◆ Quiets ◆ Quit ◆ Quivering ◆ Quixotic ◆ Quoin ◆ Quondam

Q is for Quicksilver which has a reputation for moodiness, changeability. Someone will have to tell me why. It's a shiny silver white. It's a metal, liquid at room temperature. Its atomic weight is 200.59. Its atomic number is 80. Its atomic symbol is Hg. It is very dense—lead will float in it. It has a boiling point of 675 degrees Fahrenheit, which is low. It's odorless. It has 121 neutrons. Its name derives form Old English *cwicu* (alive) and *seolfor* (silver). In more modern science, it is named for Mercury (Hermes), the messenger god.

In the form most people are familiar with, mercury dropped from a broken thermometer, it doesn't pool like water, but forms into shiny droplets, which can be swept back together to form one large shiny droplet, much like the villain in *Terminator 2*. This game is nigh on irresistible, and, when questioned, most people will tell you they've done it, even that they've kept a vial of broken thermometer quicksilver expressly for this purpose. Like a pet.

But what do most people know about quicksilver? Even those who shyly confess they've kept some as a pet? What's the main thing about quicksilver?

It is poisonous. Terribly, irreversibly poisonous. Mercury nitrates were used to turn fur into felt in the nineteenth century, a time when, like Timmy, most people wore hats. And the hatters who made that felt into hats, who dealt with quicksilver day in and day out? Well, they all went crazy. Sooner or later, enough brain damage done from handling the mercury nitrates, hatters wig out.

Sooner or later, hatters wig out. Thus the expression, mad as a hatter. Thus the common, nineteenth century disease called Hatter's Shakes in England and Danbury Shakes in the United States—Danbury, Connecticut being the center of the hat industry in this country. In the twentieth century (*twentieth to* you *maybe, but these are not my people*), dentists who made mercury fillings and those poor slobs with the pre-penicillin clap were also known for wigging out, sooner or later, from the fillings and the iatrogenic injections, respectively. Inevitably.

Quicksilver is poisonous. Sooner or later, people who handle it wig out. I find this strangely comforting.

If the thing that poisoned your mind was fatal to the healthy function of that mind, inevitably, then no one would expect you to be able to master it. Get over it. You would just be you, poisoned, delusional, quivering in the corner. You might garner an observer's pity (poor dear, she was a hatter, you know; poor dear, she loved a quixotic Irishman, you know) or even disgust (honestly, can't they *do* something about these creatures?) but you'd never be subject to boosterism. Never be directed to a quack grief support group.

None of which tells me why mercury has a reputation for changeability. Why something given to multiple, lightning changes is called quicksilver or mercurial. The best I can figure, mercury is associated with changeability not because mercury changes, but because it changes what it encounters. The best I can figure? Well, granted, that's maybe not so good, but cut me some slack. I love a quixotic Irishman. And he's dead.

Timmy, it is true, was quixotic in temperament. Single-minded in ambition, at least when I knew him, but moody and endlessly curious, given to elaborate flights of fancy. And, like a man of the nineteenth century, like a man of my people—well, like any man, at least until Kennedy's tenure, he always wore a hat.

The Irish temper is the stuff of legend. We all know it, right? Speak of it in hushed, reverent tones? But that was not Timmy's nature, exactly. His mood was volatile—well, no. *Capricious*—capering from here to there, but never violent or angry, morose or withdrawn. He would have been, I guess. Except that everything seemed too funny to him. And, of course, as Pudge always reminds me, he had his fleas.

As a casual observer, I'd have to say that people with quixotic moods tend to shack up with the vigilant sort, people who are hyper-attuned to such quicksilver changes in the emotional weather. But that was not my nature.

I was not on the *qui vive* when I was with Timmy. I wasn't a sentinel. I wasn't the keeper of order and calm. When Timmy's storms blew over me, I recognized them as storms. Ill winds or winds of grandiose, manic delight. Either way, they blew over my head. I just made quiet note of them and went about my business. I wasn't hyper-attuned, didn't try to fix or predict them.

Quixotic winds of emotion cannot be measured. And creatures of reason don't play that way.

Quicksilver loses all its electric resistance at 4.2 degrees above absolute zero. It becomes perfectly, absolutely conductive—a superconductor. Buffered with something to cool it continually, like liquid helium, mercury can keep a current flowing forever.

What can we learn from these ruminations? What is here that I can build on? Use as a quoin in a brand-spanking new cathedral of not-Timmy?

Well, nothing.

If Timmy were like quicksilver, he wouldn't have been changeable because Mercury isn't changeable. If Timmy were quicksilver as a superconductor he would have kept his current going forever, at least as long as he had a cooling agent. If Timmy were quicksilver, what would that make me? A mad hatter? Liquid helium? A broken thermometer?

What it boils down to is what every avenue of thought boils down to. Timmy made me live, quickened me, then checked out. Timmy sold me a bill of goods. There is no metaphor, no way to measure or understand what has happened. No answer which will satisfy my unasked question. No way to ask the question, quell the longing. Every avenue of pursuit leads me back to the quicksand I'm sunk in.

What it boils down to is what it always boils down to. Vapors of poisonous mercury I've already inhaled. What it boils down to is what it always boils down to.

Because Timmy is a dead hypocrite. And because all roads lead to Rome.

"Well, start with that, then," Pudge says. He is next to me on the subway. Is it the weekend again already?

"With what?"

"Dr. Acree is a dead hypocrite. What facts do you know about dead hypocrites?"

"What counts as a fact?"

"Hey, Iz. All roads lead to Rome. You claim to know a little bit about everything. What's *anything* you know about dead hypocrites?"

"The Talmud tells us that seven years after a hypocrite dies, he becomes a bat."

Pudge inhales, then exhales in bursts through his nose, as if to start laughing. His laugh is rich, gleaming, like light bouncing off mercury. He is about to say what he always says when he doesn't know what to say; when he doesn't know what to say, and saying something he *does* know—like the fact that unless under tremendous pressure, quicksilver always crystallizes in an isometric form, three axes of equal length—isn't an option.

"Please don't tell me you're just an entomologist," I say.

We are quiet and the train screeches into Carroll Street, spits us out on Smith Street. We take the long way, avoiding the highway overpass, past the projects and the park, the old grain terminal, the Erie Basin. It's a long walk. I could do it in my sleep. And maybe I am.

That line is blurry to me, now. I cannot deny that I am hunting something, but my actions are inscrutable, unfathomable, immeasurable, even to myself. There are mysteries here, for sure. But I don't think mine is among them.

Red Hook is shot through with secret passageways, underground canals and channels, leading to double basements, blind alleys with hidden manhole doors—all designed in their heyday to smuggle in black market goods. Liquor, during prohibition. Illegal immigrants. Drugs, probably. And, if H.P. Lovecraft is to be believed, swarthy Persian devil-worshippers and little kidnapped boys.

If H.P. Lovecraft is to be believed, more people entered Red Hook than ever left it by the landward side. If H.P. Lovecraft is to believed, many a soul was lost in these climes. I guess mine could be among them. Except I'm not looking for my soul. Except I don't believe in my soul.

We approach the bar from the southwest, from the Buttermilk Channel side, from the wrong end of a dead-end street, have to scale a barbed wire fence to get up on cobbled Conover. We've had to scale three fences already. Pudge rips his jeans and laughs.

Unless he is thinking about fleas or sex, or laughing gently at my sorrow, Pudge has only one thing on his mind.

"Why didn't we drive," he asks.

"We're trying to be inconspicuous."

141

"I don't buy it," he says. "We're skulking around the outskirts of Red Hook like rats. We both look like freaks. You're bringing someone you're fucking to your night job. To say nothing of it being your dead lover's home turf. We're *not* trying to be inconspicuous. So why couldn't we drive?"

"We're saving that," I say.

He is laughing as we push into the bar. The Balustrade. The Leap.

I look in the barback mirror. We *do* look like freaks. For one thing my bartender clothes are ripped and rumpled, pulled askew in several directions at once. Pudge's broken glasses, pocket protector and feathery dust mop blond hair seem grafted on the ease of his bearing, his East Asian face. He looks cobbled together of disparate parts.

I am much smaller than him. Easily half his size. The colors and curves have leeched almost completely out of me. I am ashen and angular. Titless. Crowned with clumpy hair, the color of scotch mixed with dark, clotted blood.

Mark is behind the bar, chatting up a . . . could it be? A Jersey Girl. Big blonde hair. I mean, huge. Enough hair-volume for two heads, easy. Perfect French manicure. High heels with pants. She looks like a customer at the Haunted Mansion, squealing through the webby spookhouse halls. She looks like she drives a Camaro.

Mark is wearing a suit. It fits him, but he doesn't fit it. He looks uncomfortable. Like a kid at his *bar mitzvah*. He glares at Pudge Goroguchi. He glares at me. So far so good. His customary greeting.

"Thanks for comin' in, Iz. We've got tickets and Boris is indisposed."

Indisposed? Boris? Like passed out, headfirst in an old bar-spittoon of his own puke? Or maybe he's going to a show too.

At the end of the bar, Coo laughs.

"Boris is indisposed," he says to his drinks. He has two of them, shots of whiskey.

Now Pudge laughs and Mark glares at him. So far so good. His customary response.

There is a stalemate of maybe thirty seconds' duration. We are all poised in this tableau. Thirty seconds, I know from growing up with them, is about five or even ten seconds longer than a Jersey Girl can handle silence. Got himself a deep one, Mark has.

She squeals and the moment passes. Suddenly it is old home day.

"Is this Izzy," she asks, long emphasis on the second syllable which shows off Hollywood-style capped teeth. Or maybe she was born with them. The drawn-out "zee" of Izzy turns into a squeal and she hugs me, then looks me up and down.

"Mark has told me so much about you. Haven't you, honey?"

He wipes the bar, shifts his feet. What, no glare?

"Qiana, this is Izzy," he says. It costs him something, but not too much.

At the end of the bar, Coo laughs. "Qiana, this is Izzy," he says, holding a shot glass in each fist, bowing them at each other. The left whiskey puppet squeals as he drains it.

Mark glares at him.

Qiana arranges her face in a condescending smile. I wait for it. The pointless dis. Once upon a time I could've mopped the floor with her. Now, I don't have the energy.

"Mark was telling me about his brother and your problems and all," Qiana says. She is looking at my raggy clothes.

"I was gonna say, I have some old stuff I'm giving away, but no. They're probably not your, uh, style."

She giggles.

"Anyway, you really need a figure for them. Still, you could look through them, if you like. I was just going to donate them to Goodwill."

The quondam tough girl in me wells, then quiets. I didn't know she was still in there. They are all looking at me. What for? Don't they know they can't count on me? Don't they know I'm already dead?

Fuck it. Fuck the Jersey Girl, drunk Coo, laughing Pudge, indisposed Boris. Tortured sons of the auld sod, the rising sun, the Paramus Park Mall. Fuck Timmy's memory. Fuck Mark for finding a way to live.

Fuck it.

"Well, thanks just the same, Qiana. But since you probably got your clothes off the same cheerleader who sold you your manners, I think I'll pass."

Pudge and Coo laugh. Mark glares. Qiana blinks. I don't think she gets it. She dismisses me with an empty smile.

Mark glares daggers through me. He slaps one of his giant paws on the bar.

"You can't fire me, Mark. I quit."

Now he sighs.

"Right, we'll be off, then," he says.

"Who's the laughing man?" one of Coo's whiskeys.

"Search me," says the other.

"This is Pudge Goroguchi," I say to the floor.

Mark shakes his hand. Coo offers him a whiskey. Mark unties his apron and hands it to me. He takes Qiana's arm.

"What's wrong with him," I hear her stage whisper as they exit. "Is he Chinese?"

Coo and Pudge find this hilarious. I like it, though. What's wrong with any of them? Are they Chinese? Didn't they hear me?

I quit.

18. ROAD RUNNER

Radical Rake ◆ Ranting ◆ Rapidly ◆ (Compression) Ratio ◆ Realm ◆ Rear Bulkhead ◆ Rear-end Reason ◆ Re-build ◆ Redline ◆ Responsibilities ◆ Retirement Package ◆ Revolutions Per Minute Revving ◆ Ride ◆ Ridiculous ◆ Right ◆ Risk ◆ Road Runner ◆ Rolled ◆ Rub of the Relic ◆ Running

R is for Road Runner. Pudge Goroguchi's car differs from the one in my dream, the one Timmy and Johnny Thunders left me in, only in that it is not a re-build job. Pudge's car has all the features of a dream car, *the* dream car, but, unlike the one in my dream, its features are just as they were delivered to the original owner, mere weeks before he was killed in Vietnam.

Pudge's car sat under wraps somewhere in farm country, tended to but unsullied, until the owner's father died, at which point less sentimental relatives sought to unload it. Apparently, they no longer wished to live under the spectre of their hallowed, dead cousin, killed in a war we all now agree was pointless.

This story is, in my opinion, only slightly less ridiculous than the one Timmy told in the dream. It is preposterous, almost iconic. A teen boy's wetdream, minus only the tits.

Nevertheless, it is, according to Pudge, the truth. I'm not sure what to make of it, except to say that it is the kind of thing that happens to people like Pudge Goroguchi. Or Timmy. People who have a peculiar genius for being in the right place at the right time. People for whom things always fall into place. People for whom dreams come true.

Entomologists.

In my Road Runner dream, though I know full well there is no such car, that Timmy and Johnny Thunders are just spinning this laughable story to get money for dope, I also can't help picturing the car.

It is snot-green with a black vinyl roof. It has low restricted dual exhausts, a special hood with air scoops, heavy duty suspension. It is 203.2 inches long, with a wheelbase of 115. Curiously, it has bench seats. The rear axle has a Sure-Grip differential—what GM used to call "posi-traction." Oh, and it has a 3/8 I.D. fuel line.

The 426 HEMI engine Johnny Thunders beams about in the dream has a bore of 4.25 inches and a stroke of 3.75 inches. The bigger the bore, the longer the stroke, the larger the combustion chamber, the more explosive the result. These are facts you don't need any special knowledge of cars to understand viscerally. Anyone who has ever gazed into the eyes of someone he is likely to fuck before the evening is through can understand it. Even Johnny Thunders could understand it.

425 horses at 5000 revolutions per minute in the 426 HEMI works out to a horse per cubic inch. Almost. An almost horse. 490 foot-pounds at 4000 revolutions per minute. The speed of the crankshaft, transferred to the back wheels. We're talking about a scary amount of power here. The car in my dream, the dream car, the car Timmy and Johnny Thunders plan to rent so they can drive to San Francisco to start a commune, it's no joke.

Pudge's car, as I've said, looks just like it. But even in the dream, as a picture of the car Timmy is describing coalesces before me, it never occurs to me that all the features of the car are factory-installed. Here I am thinking of that HEMI engine.

Only 55 of the 14,218 Road Runners sold in 1971 were sold with a HEMI installed. I don't know how many of those were snot green, with a black vinyl roof, Hurst four-on-the-floor, but I doubt there could be more than three or four out there. These facts were with me in the dream, as they are with me in my waking life — two states not now easily distinguishable in any case.

I have no special love of cars, but facts about cars are part of the fiber of my being. I breathe in, I breathe out, I know about cars. I am from New Jersey. I was born in the 1970s. I know about muscle cars. It is basic, essential. Primal. Like hunting for food, seeking shelter, getting my DNA selected for existence in the next generation.

I am primitive man. I know about cars.

Why this should be, I'm not sure. Maybe it's something they put in the Jersey drinking water to counteract the toxic waste.

The brutal truth is, I am not sure of much of anything. Somewhere along the line, I absorbed knowledge about cars from the ether, by osmosis. Just as somewhere along the line, I must have decided that reason was my last best hope. Not a reasonable notion, when emotions are running high, when there are questions without answers. But if clinging to sanity, to reason is itself unreasonable, insane, then what's a girl to do?

Still, since I quit showing up at The Leap, quit having to arrange my face into the face of a sad-eyed bartender, I have felt calmer. Stripping away one's contact with the world, responsibilities in it, is clearly not a reasonable course of action here, but then, neither is clinging to reason, right?

I am way over the redline here, my wheels spinning at 5250 rpm, easy. My transmission whining, then screaming. My tachometer useless, shot. But I have no gears to switch to. I am not going anywhere. At this rate, doing nothing but revving faster and faster as the fuel/air mix grows, doing nothing but revolving in place, my heart will simply explode.

As any car, even a classic American performance vehicle, even a dream car, even a car in a dream would. An engine, no matter how powerful, can only do what it was designed to do, can only operate within the parameters of that function. If forced to behave otherwise, it will, inevitably, break down. In the case of a

426 horsepower engine, explode. Inevitably.

When driving at high speed—such as in a 1971 Plymouth Road Runner, on a Jersey drag strip. Or running away, in an undernourished body built for loving someone dead—when driving at high speeds, if someone wipes out ahead of you, the safest, most reasonable course of action is to aim straight for the wreck. By the time you get there, it will have moved. If you swerve to avoid the wreck, you risk driving right into the sliding conflagration.

That's what they say, and I guess it makes pretty good sense. Unless of course you happen to be both the driver and the wreck up ahead. In which case, what? In which case we are transported back to that realm of parlor-trick New Physics I never really felt at home in.

I never felt at home anywhere except in Timmy's arms, but what's the difference? I know, Mark knows, Pudge knows, the people on the street who avoid me with sliding eyes know, the ranting pitside frat boys know, I am headed straight for the wreck. It is only a matter of time. And time, on the quarter mile, at soul-crushing speeds, is short.

And thus, I am calmer. I know what's coming. It only stands to reason. Reason—which is not the same as sanity or morality. But reason has certain compensatory advantages. It's a tool of prediction. And once you know what's coming, inevitably, there is no reason to stand against it, resist it.

And thus, I am calmer. It is as if, as the possible futures narrow in scope, I have more and more energy for those few possibilities which remain. And calmer, more energy, these things . . . are good.

My hands are stars on the grubby floor, the weight in my wrists, bony like fish. My ass and legs are way up on the bed, with Pudge who is, *plus ça change*, fucking me. The position is not unfamiliar to me. Timmy liked it sometimes, not for fucking but for watching, for visuals as he had, as he said, a rub of the relic.

But cars more than Timmy, more than Pudge's grinding machinations, are on my mind and I laugh, as the position's secret face reveals itself to me. Not secret. Basic. Essential. What the authors of the *Kama Sutra* might've called it, if they'd had crank shafts and heat engines back when that impenetrable sex manual got penned.

"What's so goddamn funny, Iz?"

"Pudgeman, I believe you have finally realized your boyhood dream."

"Bagging a scrawny banker?"

"No. A radical rake."

And we have. Jacked-up rear-end, the hallmark of muscle car aerodynamics, the subsequent increase in speed, force and torque. And then, of course, there's the look. If your ride has a rake, you're driving power. Thus, the muscle geek's favorite tag-line—Move Over. Power Approaching Rapidly.

The 1971 Plymouth Road Runner, I suppose it should be noted, was not exactly, in its day, a cool car. It marked the beginning of the end of that era, and the stink of the death of the factory hotrod was already upon it. The price was back up, the car came loaded with comfort options which made purists blanch. Carpeting, rear side windows which rolled down. As if someone might be in there, right? Well, who? Your junior high daughter, the soccer fiend?

The 1971 Plymouth Road Runner was already showing the weight of the changing times. The oil embargo, emissions standards. Insurance regs, a down-sized compression ratio. The car was, as Eamon "Flattop" O'Leary, the big heap musclehead of Watsessing Elementary liked to say, fat. Fat, right? Not phat. This *is* 1971 we're talking about here. Fat, as in lumbering, too well-fed, ponderous. Its Satellite body, already boxy like a Notre Dame footballer's, now laden with gimcracks, like a retired Notre Dame footballer's gut after fifteen years of beer.

I do not mean to say that Pudge's car is not cool. It is incredibly cool. And I do not mean to say that Pudge's car is not powerful. It is impossibly powerful. And it is a classic. And it is a beauty. But given a choice no one now gets, between owning a 1971 Plymouth Road Runner and owning, say, a 1969 Plymouth Road Runner, your typical musclehead would opt for the '69. Pudge knows this, and I think he likes it. It is endearing to love a car, and it is endearingly eccentric to love a car that strives for perfection, but fails, just short of the mark.

I am smoking, my upper body still on the floor, when he says it.

"I've been invited to Australia to head up a five-year research project on the Bolivian Thorn Forest tapeworm."

"That would seem to make no sense."

"Yeah, well, that's what makes it so exciting. We're talking about a species that predates the current land-mass formations."

"What about the artificial dog?"

"Oh, I'm sure Dr. Guetta will be happy to buy me out. He suspects me of sabotaging the client base among the pest control companies in order to protect the fleas."

"Is it true?"

"Not the way he means."

I am quiet, taking this in. I heave my upper body back up on the bed. I reach over Pudge to grind out the cigarette. He is grinning. And, like with Coogan, a conspiracy forms whole in mind.

As if it were always there and I, just then, ran into it.

"What about your car?" I say.

He runs his hands though his dust-mop hair and looks, for

the first time ever, serious.

"I guess I have to sell it," he says. "I don't know who to, though. I paid $65,000 for it. And I've put another ten grand in."

"There must be people willing to pay $75,000 for a car like that."

"Sure," he says, "but I don't know if I can find one in five weeks."

"Five weeks?"

"Uh-huh."

"$75,000?"

"Uh-huh."

The moment, worth narrating, I guess, although I have nothing new to add to the collected human responses to such moments, shimmers. The moment shimmers, I shiver, and everything is clear.

"My 401-K is worth that much," I say.

He turns to me, takes my face in his long white hands, chuckles sweetly. Hanging in the air between us is what he ought to say, but cannot. That I need my retirement money for my retirement. That that's what retirement packages are *for*.

"Can you even drive it, Izzy?"

"Does that matter?"

He sighs, looks at the window-space boarded up with medium-density fiberboard and sheetrock and muslin—and, finally, predictably, laughs.

"At least once, darlin'," he says. "I don't want anyone else to get hurt."

I bound out of the bed, startling Airshaft.

"Let me show you," I say.

He laughs and gropes around on the floor for his clothes.

We sit in the car. I put the clutch in, shift into neutral. I rest my foot lightly on the accelerator, push it to the floor and release it. Pudge looks on approvingly. I turn the ignition key and the engine roars to life. Because I cannot resist, I tap the accelerator with my foot and the whole car torques clockwise.

"Can we go to Jersey," I ask as I put my foot on the brake, release the handbrake, ram my right hand up into first.

"I'm just—"

"Don't say it," I holler, as I gradually shift my brakefoot to the accelerator, begin to push down, letting the clutch up.

"—the passenger," he finishes.

19. SACKED

Sacked ✦ Safe ✦ Sanatorium ✦ (Belt) Sander ✦ Satanic Chapel ✦ Scotch Drawer ✦ Scrawled
Second ✦ Sense of Security ✦ Sergeant ✦ Shareholder ✦ Shifted ✦ Shrieked ✦ Side ✦ Simple
Slipping ✦ Sorry ✦ Spanish ✦ Spiel ✦ Squeezed ✦ Steady ✦ Stock Transfer ✦ Strings ✦ Syllables

S is for Sacked. The first time I was fired, it was unfair. I loved my job at the Haunted Mansion at Long Branch and I was good at it. Although, as I've said, I liked the headless man rig best, liked slipping into the turtleneck/funnel/mirror contraption and quietly watching the patrons in the mirrored ceiling, I was fully capable in all the roles.

Our roles weren't scripted, each of us working out the spiel that suited our temperament—or mood of the moment. As the mad rat professor, facing a group of patrons who had just walked though a pitch-black narrow corridor, over tens of thousands of pieces of cut garden hose, squeaking and leaping under their feet, I liked to scamper frantically, and twitch, pitch my voice to a squeak, mutter impossible, disjointed syllables, half rat myself.

When Donna, an actual midget, who played a dead midget, went on a two-week sick leave to be deloused, I was the only one willing to lie in her coffin, risking a lice-infestation myself. I was good at my job, and I liked it. I was a trooper. In all my years there, I only broke character twice.

The first time, I was working as an extra, cowled, delivering water in severed-head jugs to the other employees. We had a code system, although it always struck me that hearing "we have a code five in the Satanic Chapel" over an intercom was just as likely to

153

spoil the illusion as hearing *anything* over an intercom. Code five meant someone was freaking out, which happened fairly regularly. Code four meant that someone important had entered the spookhouse, which usually meant a member of the Miano family. The Mianos owned the pier, were rumored to be heavily connected, and were suspected of ordering the fire which eventually burned the Haunted Mansion at Long Branch to ashes.

The first time I broke character, I was delivering water to Chris Johnson as he sat in the headless man rig. The intercom buzzed and crackled, and the manager's distorted voice reverberated through the room.

"We have a code four," she said, and his face safe behind the mirror, Chris rolled his eyes.

"Repeat," the intercom crackled again, "we have a code four."

"Code four," the manager's voice now slightly hysterical.

"Code four. And it's Lou Rawls."

With that, Chris Johnson and I broke into peals of such irrepressible laughter that we were still laughing when Lou Rawls came in, which only made us laugh harder. We never heard anything about it, so I doubt Lou Rawls' spookhouse experience was effected one way or the other.

Breaking character was, in and of itself, not grounds for dismissal. The manager loved the spookhouse, and seemed to view us rather as a frontline combat sergeant views his troops. Besides, she had a steady side business selling acid to the customers, with which moonlighting she was no doubt stepping on the drug-distribution network of someone connected to the Mianos themselves, so I doubt she wanted to rock the boat.

The second time I broke character, I was in the Satanic Chapel, again cowled, mumbling, worshipping at the altar. The Satanic Chapel was the most elaborate and effective of the mansion's rooms. It was built right out over the ocean, was, as a result, dank, dripping and cold, scrawled over with mysterious lettering, creepy pentagrams, backwards Latin imprecations—the works. Horrible deep chimes tolled on the soundtrack, fronted by incomprehensible whispering chants and the occasional scream. To top it off, the Satanic Chapel featured an animatronic devil effigy, which shifted alarmingly whenever a wave hit the pier outside.

On my last day of work at the Haunted Mansion, a middle-aged Dominican woman entered the Satanic Chapel, crossed herself, and promptly wigged out. This wasn't an unusual occurrence; we even, remember, had a code for it, which I issued, as I pushed back the cowl, and went to comfort her.

My removal of the cowl only made her wail more fiercely, and she fell, twisting her ankle, and began to scrabble away from me, praying. My Spanish was iffy, the kind picked up living on the streets of a mixed neighborhood rather than polished by a semester in Barcelona, but best as I could figure, she seemed to feel that everything I was saying was just what a minion of the devil would say, if trying to give her a false sense of security before delivering her soul to my master.

When the manager and Donna the midget, wig askew, rushed in, the woman shrieked and lost consciousness. By the time she was revived in the ambulance, she was threatening a lawsuit.

The case never made it to court, but we had an internal investigation, headed up by some humorless corporate apologist hired by the Mianos. The apologist asked me, seemingly in all seriousness, whether I worshipped the devil. To which I responded "I don't even *believe* in the devil," which was apparently the wrong thing to say. His recommendation was that they fire me as a conciliatory gesture to the community. The manager argued in my favor, the rest of staff offered petitions and testimonials, and Donna the midget cried when I picked up my last check. But there was no redemption for me.

And now *I* am employed as a corporate apologist.

Or rather, I was.

In my years as an Immolator for the Stock Transfer Complaints Defects Correspondents in the Tenders and Exchanges Department of the Interstate Bank of New York and New Jersey, I have responded to many letters. And as I grind out the mollifying response, the response I'd like to write forms in my head. I do not send this version, you understand, I only draft it in my head.

Years of doing this, day in and day out, leaving Timmy in a warm bed, his briny sleep smell like a baby's head, but with balls—then months of leaving that same bed cold, unmade—years of doing this led me to wonder, often enough, what kind of stock transfer complaint letter would finally break me, force me to respond authentically.

What flavor of stock transfer insanity would finally force my hand? Take it by the wrist and lead it to draft a letter which would of course get me fired, but would be worth it, because, in that one brief instance, I'd be telling the truth? How hateful would the letter have to be? How psychotic? How ugly and scrawled? How full of narrow-minded greed? Twisted world views? Choked anti-Semitism?

And what would my response be like? How clever and cutting? How full of knife-blade prose and vast expanses of sad? I pictured myself, every day I pictured myself, going out laughing, in a blaze of prole glory.

But the letter that got me fired was none of these.

Dear Sirs: I will explain to you. A white lady gave me these ten shares of your stock once when I helped her with her bags outside Puffy's. I didn't think nothing of it since I am an old man with diabetes and one leg and people are kind and give me lots of things whatever they have to spare even if they are not right in the head themself. Last week at the infirmary kitchen a young man told me his story of how his dead father had sent him all these belt sanders from your company broken but maybe if fixed up they could be worth something. The belt sanders was a legacy, they call it. The boy is slow and I do not think he could figure out the repairs himself and since he asked me what he didn't meet before, I worry that maybe he will trust somebody with them who means to put one over on him. The belt sanders is not much but this is what the boy's father left him, and they is his responsibility now. He is terrible worried someone will take them and is bringing them with him in three shopping carts tied together wherever he goes which makes people think he not right in the head and maybe also not a good bet for day labor or what have you. So, I was wondering if since the belt sanders was made by your company and I am what they call a shareholder in same you might be able to advise.

Sincerely,
Pedro Diez

I read it. Then I read it again. The pathos, who'd have thought, froze me in my tracks. The pathos, the quiet respect, finished me off. I handed it to a passing colleague who scanned it, shook his head and handed it back. Which is when it hit me—there's nothing funny about that letter.

The proper response to a letter of that ilk goes a little something like this:

A copy of your letter was referred to our department. The Interstate Bank of New York and New Jersey is the Transfer Agent for Swingcorp Common Stock. We maintain the company's shareholder records, transfer the company's shares, and pay its dividends.

However, our bank is not itself part of Swingcorp. Our area of expertise is not maintaining or repairing Swingcorp appliances, and for that reason we suggest that you redirect your questions about Swingcorp belt sanders to the company's customer service hotline at 1-800 -SWI-NGCO.

If you need assistance with any aspect of your Swingcorp Common Stock account, which contains ten (10) shares, please contact one of our telephone representatives at this toll-free number . . .

Simple enough, right? Except that I couldn't write it. Because nothing about Pedro Diez's letter was funny to me. And, if she's to keep at it, year after year, that's the way an Immolator does her job.

What's funny here? The internal theme music of the stock transfers complaints and defects maven. Ask yourself, keep asking yourself, what's funny here?

I brought the letter to my immediate supervisor, the vice president in charge of stock transfer complaints and defects letters in the department of tenders and exchanges, who read it and looked up. At me, then at the bank-approved Musée D'Orsay print behind me.

She shrugged.

"What's a belt sander," she said.

Is the question funny, I thought. Yes. Now, *that's* a funny question. Good. I can answer a funny question.

"A belt sander is small power tool. Picture an iron, the handle mounted on a base containing a motor with two drive wheels. Flat on the bottom to accommodate a belt maybe two inches wide and two feet long. The base of the sander is about ten inches. The motor spins the belt between two drums mounted horizontally—"

"Ms. Oytsershifl, do you have a specific problem with this letter?"

"Yes. I don't know how to respond to it."

She shook her head.

"I'm afraid I don't understand. Why?"

"There's nothing funny about it."

She sighed and put the letter down, went over its creases slowly, with a lacquered thumbnail.

"You know, I'm glad you brought this to my attention. Your efficiency has been falling off dramatically for the past eight months."

"Tell me about it."

"Now, I know you've been having some problems at home, but do you really expect your colleagues to carry you forever?"

Is that a *funny* question, I thought. Yes. Good. I can answer a funny question.

"No. I do not expect my colleagues to carry me forever."

She leaned in conspiratorially, arranged her face in a ghastly warm smile.

"You know, when I was having," she dropped her voice to a whisper, "the change?" She took my hand. "I just couldn't deal, you know? My sister took me to this," she dropped into a sub-whisper, "sanatorium?" She took both our hands in her other hand and squeezed. "They gave me some happy pills, fixed me right up. I know you've, uh, used up all your paid leave, but if you'd consider an unpaid leave, maybe I could pull some strings. Do you think you'd like that, Ms. Oytsershifl?"

Is that a funny question? Do I think I'd like to take an unpaid leave and go to a sanatorium to get some happy pills? Do I think I'd like that? Is that a funny question? Yes, I guess it is. Good. I can answer funny questions.

"No," I said, withdrawing my hand from her ministrations. "I don't think that would help."

Tears sprung to her eyes.

"I'm sorry you feel that way," she said.

"So am I," I said.

"I think the bank has been more than generous with you, Ms. Oytsershifl. But if you're going to take that attitude, I'm afraid you're beyond my help."

"Oh, I think I'm way beyond your help."

She pulled open her right bottom drawer, the scotch drawer, except that hers was filled with forms. One of which she folded into an envelope. She sealed the envelope and painstakingly wrote my name in calligraphy on the outside. This she handed me gravely.

"Please consider Friday your last day here. Take this envelope to personnel on your lunch hour."

"Okay," I said.

"I really tried to extend myself to you, Ms. Oytsershifl. You realize that, don't you?"

Is that a funny question? Not really. I stood quietly, looking at her.

She sighed.

"Well, I hope you know I'll fight any requests for unemployment benefits. I mean, it's not as if I didn't try."

"It's not as if I didn't try either."

"If you don't mind my saying so, Ms. Oytsershifl. It doesn't seem like you're trying at all."

"I don't mind your saying so. Everyone does."

On the way back to my desk, I passed the fat man, still engrossed in his dog-eared Gibbon. His eyes took in the envelope, the calligraphy.

"Pink slip?"

I nodded.

"Yeah, you got that look."

I nodded again.

"Tell me about it," I said.

He regarded me for a moment, with a look that was at once

amused and grave.

"What's wrong with you, Oyster?"

Oyster. Thirteen years across a two-foot gray aisle from one another and today, he gives me a nickname. My childhood nickname. My school-lot nickname. My *street* name, if you will. The only other person who ever called me "Oyster" as an adult was—well, why dwell on it?

What's that he asked me?

Is it a *funny* question?

"What's wrong with me?"

He nodded.

"I'm Chinese."

He nodded again, as if that were answer.

The first time I was fired, it wasn't my fault. The second time, I suppose it was. But it all evens out in the wash, right?

It's not as if I'll need the unemployment benefits.

Tails ✦ Takhrikhim ✦ Tam ✦ Tampon Museum ✦ Tangible ✦ Taxonomy ✦ Taylor Ham
There ✦ Thoughts ✦ Thumbs ✦ (Johnny) Thunders ✦ Tifkayt ✦ Times ✦ Timmy ✦ Titillations
Today ✦ Too Late ✦ Top Hat ✦ Toyt ✦ Trenches ✦ Trousseau House ✦ Troyer ✦ Tsedreyt

T is for Timmy.

Timmy.

Timmy. Timmy.

Timmy. Timmy. Timmy.

Tsegezetst zol er vern vayl ikh hob im in tokhes.

May he blow up, since I've got him up my ass anyway. Too late for that sentiment. Though I suppose I could shove the charred remains of him up my ass. They've been in all my other orifices. I could wire them as explosives, and shove them up my ass. And blow them up.

But no. It's too late for that sentiment.

Too late.

Timmy. T is for Timmy. The thing about Timmy, he didn't become ethereal until he was dead. I search for him and search for him, trying on metaphor after metaphor. Solid metaphors. Tangible metaphors. Metaphors of the physical world. Metaphors I can bite. But to no avail. Timmy is ghostly, elusive. Timmy's essence is vague and yet, for me, inchoate.

Well, as it should be, right? Because Timmy's dead.

T is for Timmy's dead.

But Timmy wasn't like that when he was alive. Not dead, of course. And not ethereal. He wasn't the kind of man whose nature or thoughts were elusive. He wasn't the kind of man who answered every question with a speech about what kind of man he was.

I do not mean to say he wasn't, as we used to say, deep. Or that he wasn't at home in the symbolic realms of artistry. Of course he was. But Timmy was a guy who was always where his body was. Timmy was a body, with a whip-smart mind at its helm.

When he was alive, before he became dead, and ethereal, Timmy was a body. And wherever that body was, so too was his attention. Right there in the moment. Right there in the trenches with you, or his fleas, or his audience. Or whomever he was with. He was there. In the flesh. All of him. Present and accounted for.

Oh, he spoke with the silver (mercurial?) tongue of his people. He was a great fan of malarkey. Blarney. Baloney. Flights of fancy. Awful puns. (Actually, the puns were often quite good. It's just that I'm a creature of reason and all puns are awful to me, don't flip my skirt.) I don't mean to say that he spoke only of the tangible, the real. But when it came to himself, to reports from the depths, he was a reliable stringer.

He knew exactly what he wanted and pursued it ferociously. He knew how close he was to those goals and when he had to adjust them. Nothing about his internal weather had to be guessed, inferred, intuited. When Timmy was a body, present and alive, he was always there.

He was a force to be reckoned with, for sure. A gale force. But he was there for the reckoning with. That was his essential nature. Presence. How do you reckon with the absence of such a thing?

Timmy.

Timmy = presence.

Timmy gone.

I don't know, man. How do you *reckon* with such a thing?

Timmy. Timmy dressed up for a performance, in his tails and top hat, green eyes aglitter, was almost more than the heart could bear. Timmy's thumbs were long and he could bend them back to his wrist. Timmy loved chive and ate it with everything. Timmy's deep laugh filled all the space between you and him, drew you in. You could hear it with your body like a bass line at a rock concert.

Timmy. Timmy secretly preferred Boddington's to Guinness. He doted on fleas. He loved Mark's crusty prole-ishness, and Boris's drunkenness and my fanatical devotion to reason. He was always delighted when things and people acted in accordance with their nature. His own nature was, as I've said, one of presence.

Timmy. Shake your head sadly now. Timmy.

All that's left of him now is his absence. But that absence is huge. It fills up all the space around me. Encroaches into that space daily. I am smaller and smaller in its awesome presence. The presence of the absence. How do you *reckon* with something like that?

One thing's for sure. As the absence grows, I shrink. And as I shrink, there is less and less of me to do the reckoning. But when his absence eats me completely, and I disappear, I will do it with more grace than Timmy. I will disappear completely.

And I will take my absence with me.

What then will be left? Well, I don't know. Rarefied sophistry was never my long suit. But here's what I suspect: when I disappear, what will be left will be the absence of Timmy.

But at least I won't have to reckon with it.

T is for *di tifkayt*, profundity. T is for *di tayve*, lust. T is for *di takhrikhim*, burial shrouds. T is for *der troyer* and *der tsaar* which both mean grief. T is for *tsedreyt* and *tsetumlt* which both mean confused. T is for *toyt*, dead. T is for *der tam*, moron. Half-wit. *Der tam*, that's me. T is for me.

T is for Timmy. Timmy, to put the best possible spin on it, is with God now. How ridiculous that sounds. I cannot even imagine the person it would comfort. Well, God maybe. Maybe it would comfort God. To know that he has Timmy with him. Timmy.

Timmy angel.

Angels generally make their appearance toward the end. But I've long since given up hope that Timmy will appear. Now, or toward the end. Now that we are toward the end now.

Close your eyes and wait for Timmy. Count to three and he will appear.

He will not appear.

Not Timmy. Not Timmy; Timmy negated. Timmy negated will appear.

How would he come if he came, do you think? In Pudge's car, my car soon. Angel Timmy in the dream car, but having long since kicked Johnny Thunders' skinny ass to the curb. Peel-out marks on Howard Street, I'd leap in with him and go. Go where? Who cares? Go low-riding with Timmy angel.

Timmy angel would not have wings. Not when fleas don't. Fleas are wingless, apterous. They hop. Leap. A Timmy might kill himself, as some fleas in captivity do; they go on hunger strikes, refuse to move, eat the birdlime they are fastened with, die. A Timmy might kill himself, but a Timmy angel would never mock his apterous children by appearing with wings. No way. A Timmy angel would have *class*.

What is the taxonomy of a classy Timmy angel? Timmy angels are any of a number of small wingless hopping ghost guides who don't appear in time. Timmy angels are perpetually late, too late, like the White Rabbit. Timmy angels never come on time. But man, can they hop. Hop doesn't even cover it. Timmy angels *sproing*.

I took Timmy driving in Jersey lots of times. We visited my

mother. We went to lots of go-go bars. We went to Titillations, the go-go bar that used to be the Dirt Club that used to be a go-go bar, home of junkie entrepreneur Johnny Dirt and his dancer wife Mrs. Dirt, who invented the go-go brunch. (Timmy fixed the go-go swing with his Swiss Army knife and Mrs. Dirt cried.)

We covered Outcast New Jersey, from stem to stern. We went to Captain Al's Harbor Casino in Jersey City. Captain Al's is neither on the water, nor a casino. Just an old bar. Captain Al, it turned out, knew Timmy's father—and owed him money from a poker game, which he paid off in free drinks for us.

I took Timmy to all the best make-out spots in Palisades Park. I took Timmy *in* all the best make-out spots in Palisades Park. Timmy sucked my eyelids at one of the scenic outlooks in Alpine. Timmy shaved my armpits in the Raceway Motel at Raceway Park.

I took Timmy to see the Newark Bears, and for Portuguese food on Ferry Street and for greasy Scots fish and chips at the Argyle in Kearny. I took Timmy to the Piney Cathedral in South Mountain Reservation. To the Haunted Golf Course in Toms River. To Weeping Clown Rock in Manunkachunk, where the local sheriff killed his own wife as a re-election stunt. To the tampon museum in Denville. To Whitman's sister's Trousseau House outside Camden.

Timmy and I went driving in Jersey lots of times. We laced Wawa coffee with bourbon and drank it from a thermos while Timmy serenaded the Pine Barrens. We bought pounds of Taylor Ham and fed it all to the seagulls on Long Beach Island. We dragged a drunken DJ, sputtering from the ocean foam, out of a riptide at Asbury Park. (He said he'd gone in after a mermaid.)

Timmy and I went driving in Jersey lots of times. But we never went in a 1971 Plymouth Road Runner, sub-lime green with a black vinyl roof. With a HEMI. Hurst 4. Pop-up air grabber.

We never went in my new car.

I wish Timmy had lived to see my new car. I wish Timmy had stayed to see my new car. I wish he hadn't left me for Johnny Thunders in my new car.

See Timmy, Timmy negated, Timmy angel. See Timmy pull up in my new car. See me leap in, strap in, put my hand on his crotch. See him touch my cheek with his knuckles, pull a flea from my hair. Hear him sing—croon—over the ground-shaking, bone-quaking raw roaring song of my new car. Tim Acree. Tim *Mo Chroí*. Tim o' my heart.

Timmy and I went driving in Jersey a lot. It was all I had to show him. My car prowess. (Thank Eamon "Flattop" O'Leary for that. Flattop, king of the Essex County Motorheads, who gave driving lessons for sex.) My car prowess and my erstwhile home state. Timmy gave me everything—and I gave him Jersey.

But Jersey—and my driving prowess—was all I had. So I gave him everything, too.

Everything, New Jersey.

Aluminum Foundry, New Jersey.

Oh last night, New Jersey.

Most often, we went to Bloomfield to visit my mother. And Bloomfield, well, Bloomfield isn't much. Nail salons. Bird-faced teenagers. MSG counters. Lots of big hair. My mother, while she was alive. Sports bars and phony Irish pubs which made even Timmy long for The Balustrade.

Bloomfield isn't much. But in Bloomfield there is Willow Street, the street where I grew up. The street where my mother lived until she died. And Willow Street—as it passes the house I grew up in and my mother died in, the house that was an A&P until it became our house, with closets that always smelled of wilted lettuce—Willow Street bends into a gentle dogleg as it passes my ancestral home.

And then Willow Street runs into a wall. A huge cement wall. The supporting wall for the Garden State Parkway which runs through Bloomfield like embalming fluid.

Bloomfield isn't much. But in Bloomfield, there is Willow Street where I grew up. Willow Street in Bloomfield, New Jersey, where I grew up, it isn't much. To say the least. But Willow Street dead-ends into a wall. A huge cement wall.

Bloomfield, New Jersey.

Hometown, New Jersey.

Not much, New Jersey.

I took Timmy driving in New Jersey more times than I now remember. Timmy and I covered New Jersey from stem to stern. But I never drove Timmy to see the Willow Street wall.

If Timmy appeared as an angel, but wingless, if he peeled onto Howard Street in my new car, honked that meep-meep horn; if I leapt into the car, grinning, kissing his face all over, grabbing his crotch; if he laughed and said "where to this time? . . ."

I could take him there. Driving in New Jersey. Today we're gonna visit someplace new. Something we haven't seen before. Something you folks are gonna find really special. On today's excursion, we're gonna explore a little place called

Cement Wall, New Jersey.

Do you see where I'm going with this?

21. Ungainly

Ugly ◆ Uh, Daryl ◆ Umberto's ◆ Umbrella ◆ Umeshiso Paste ◆ Uncle Willy ◆ Unfair ◆ Ungainly
Ungepotchket ◆ Unloading (a Cat) ◆ Uplifting ◆ Upswing ◆ Urine Jug ◆ Usual ◆ Uvula

U is for ungainly, which a human life is. Ungainly, which a human body is. Carting them around—the body, and its life—is a drag. Awkward and ungainly. *Es shlept vi goles*, a human life. Drags itself out like the exile.

Deciding you soon won't have to, on the other hand; deciding that the exile's almost over, is uplifting, which U is also for. Uplifting, thrilling.

Suddenly, paradoxically, everything seems possible. Buying a new car. Giving away a dead lover's effects. Unloading a cat. Suddenly, paradoxically, U is for the upswing.

Decide you soon won't have to, and you are on the upswing.

Bounding out of bed, down the front steps, with clean hair and leather boy-hip jeans that haven't fit me since I was fifteen, I run into Uncle Willy who's packing a double-armload of government cheese.

"Whoa, there, Missy," he says. "Like my Big Mama used to say, go slowly when you're in a hurry."

I turn and laugh. Cheesy wisdom from the Government Cheeseman. Women's magazine horoscopes. Work-letter bathos. Mark's sad eyes. My mother's stupid last words. Fools who want me to suffer them gladly. Timmy unburied, powder Timmy in a jar in Brooklyn . . .

They can't none of them hurt me now.

"Thanks, Uncle Willy. That's good advice. Know how you say it in Latin?"

He smiles, widely, gently. He thinks I'm coming back to life. I am fooling him, everyone.

"*Festina lente*," I say.

"*Festina* who?"

"*Festina lente*. Make haste slowly."

He doesn't really care, but he thinks I do and makes a show of it.

"Well, I'll be. No kidding? *Festina lente*, I'm gonna have to remember that."

I have so much energy, ants in my pants, I jog in place as we chat.

I bounce.

"Think your kids would want any of Timmy's things, Uncle Willy?"

Now there is genuine joy in his eyes. He thinks I am getting over it. He thinks, at long last, I am getting over it.

"Well, if they don't, the church surely will."

"Good, I'll bring them by after supper. Have a nice day."

And I am gone. Running down the steps, up the street. I blow a kiss to Mr. Sing, the ten-thousand-year-old herbalist who keeps sweeping. I flash the guys at Algo Dye Works some serious booty. They whistle appreciatively.

I am running. And bouncing. I am full of life, lit from within, a joy to behold. I buy awful comic books from a newsstand on Centre Street and pass them out on line at the DMV. The line moves like sludge. Everyone is happy for the distraction.

Three hours later I am the official owner of a sub-lime green 1971 Plymouth Road Runner. With a black vinyl roof. Hurst four-on-the-floor. And, of course, a HEMI.

I don't have the car in my possession yet. I won't need it 'til the weekend. But I am its owner.

It is Wednesday. I have so much to do, I am flying. I am so full of wherewithal, I am flying. I pack Timmy's clothes for Uncle Willy; pack most of my own and leave them stashed by the bed. I get a Brazilian wax, a chrome-plated pedicure. I box up my parent's Jew-accoutrements—things neither Uncle Willy's brood of lost boys nor the church to which they belong will want—prayer books, *talaysim*, yarmulkes and candelabras—bring them to the nearest Temple.

I take the PATH train out to Jersey City, buy two bottles of Bacanora Real from the backroom of a Paulus Hook Mexican joint. I amble down to the ferry landing, take a good hard look at the New York skyline, shining across the lower Hudson. It is evening, Wednesday evening, and still too light for stars or lit windows.

I disembark on the New York side. Night is beginning to fall. Wednesday night. I prowl my way uptown, slowly. My feet, anyway, are moving slowly. But it is Wednesday night. Wednesday night and I have so much to do. Wednesday night—and inside me, I am flying.

I stop off at home, lug some of Timmy's stuff over to Uncle Willy's. Fuz comes back with me for the second load, takes a shine to Airshaft, pets him, kisses him. Airshaft is happy for the attention, cheeks his legs. Somehow, we convince Uncle Willy that Fuz and the other kids need a cat, something to nurture, love.

"Don't you need that too, Izzy?" Uncle Willy asks, his empathy tentacles reaching out to strangle me.

"Well, sure," I say.

I can do anything. Fool anyone. I am flying.

"But yesterday in my grief support group—"

I look up shyly. He nods.

"—they were talking about how rewarding it is just to . . . give."

Uncle Willy smiles. Looks over at his foster kids huddled around Airshaft.

"What's his name," a buck-toothed kid asks.

"Uh, Daryl," I say and the deal is clinched.

I slither into a green suede jacket and go back out into the night. Wednesday night and I am flying.

Wandering.

Flying.

I buy a half pound of the best lox Russ and Daughters has (Eastern Gaspe) and linger at a newsstand on Houston, eating it with my hands, licking my fingers. A man in his seventies, in a tweed cap and trench coat, approaches the newsstand, buys a *Yiddish Forward* with pennies, hobbles away.

I follow him, mildly curious. For no particular reason, I follow him. It is Wednesday night, now quite late. I am stealthy. I am flying. I can do no wrong. I can do no other.

The old man stops at the door of an Irish pub on lower Mulberry Street. An old cop bar. A wave of loathing and nausea hits me. I don't want to see an old Jewish man go into an Irish pub.

Timmy's father, meet my father, right? I don't want to think like that anymore.

But I hold the door for him, offer him the last of my lox, which he accepts, gravely. Timmy's father, meet my father. It is Wednesday night and I am flying. I don't want to think like that anymore.

The bar door closes. I kneel and vomit. Timmy's father, meet my father. My father, who that very well could be. Or else, more likely not. Of my father, I have learned almost nothing. And now

I'm not likely to.

So it's more like, Timmy's mother, meet my father. Of Timmy's mother, we learn almost nothing. She smelled like lavender sachet, the boys say. Said. She had only two modes—off and holler. Timmy and Mark drew a caricature of her, a uvula with cross and claddagh.

I stand and backhand the vomit off my face, wipe it off my leather jeans, suck it from my hair. Knock back a good swallow of Bacanora Real.

It is Wednesday night, and I have much to do. Anyhow, the whole thing is stupid. My father's probably dead. Like my mother. Like Timmy's father and mother. Like Timmy himself.

Parents. In the end (or even the beginning) they check out. Or else they die. In the end (or even the beginning) they can't help us or save us.

Parents. True Loves. In the end they check out. Or else they die. Or else both. Parent and True Love—I am neither to nobody. When I die, I will leave no one who needs me.

A hollow victory, you say? Slim pickin's? Well, so what? On these narrow margins, I make my stand. When I die, I will leave no one who needs me. When I die, no one will be hurt. When I die, no one will have to take it like a man.

But to pull that off, I'm gonna need traffic cones.

At least three of them. Luckily, I am in New York City. Downtown in New York City. Late on a Wednesday night. Someone within a ten block radius of where I stand, covering the pool of my puke with greasy lox paper, is setting up for filming tomorrow. It is Wednesday night and I am on the prowl, flying, looking for a lonely parking P.A.

I find her at Columbus Park, where the Five Points once were. She is young and broody, with high cheekbones, hunched in a folding lawn chair, reading by flashlight. She casts nervous glances around her, as if she were in the Five Points of old, about to be hit with a bottle, her corpse robbed and defiled. She is dressed the part. The part of someone nervous and out of place, trying to fit in. Hoody and Knicks cap. Carhartt jacket, giant Levis. Kick-ass construction boots. Pure I-Be-Bad chic.

I approach her, offer the fresh bread I just cadged off Umberto's bakery on Elizabeth Street. It is four in the morning. She is bored, lonely, making minimum wage guarding parking places for big-heap filmies. I am a tiny woman, white, ten years her senior, identifiably middle-class and safe. And cool. Bearing wonderfully fragrant baked goods. It doesn't take much to get her talking.

She is cold, from sitting all night. As we speak, she squeezes the top of an orange traffic cone. I covet it, the cone. I need it and two more besides. I need them desperately. It is my raison d'etre. I try not to look, as she fondles the tip. Squeezes it flat in her hand. But I can't help myself.

She follows my eyes as we speak, feels she must explain. She is shivering, and full of resentment. Her boss has just come by, told her she must always hold a traffic cone, in case someone comes by and feels she's not earning her keep.

I am sympathetic and she warms up to me, telling me in outraged tones about the project. It is an original cable series about a band of misfit billionaire-detectives. In the episode they are shooting tomorrow, three of the leads—a tough midget, a blind optical engineer and the lady in black, who carries a silk umbrella as a trademark—bust an unfairly incarcerated tree surgeon out of the Tombs.

I laugh with her. Yes, the show is stupid. Yes, the leads are fake-looking, ugly. Yes, money is the root of all evil. Yes, people suck.

This is my entry. I tell her I'm an installation artist, a

prankster. I draw her in. Together, we break into her boss's Isuzu Trooper and arrange a little tableau.

Strap the bottles of Evian spray and the gallon jug of no-time-to-stop-and-pee urine into the seat belts. Make a mosaic peace sign of the bottles of herbal remedies. Make clothes of fast-food wrappers for all the empty quarts of oil. Break the hinges on each of thirteen clipboards.

I jimmy the glove compartment and root around in it. *Ungepotchket*, as my mother used to say. A jumbled mess. But then, most glove compartments are, right? Registration papers and maps and coffee-soiled napkins. But this is something special. *Ungepotchket* to the max, as it were.

In among the usual assortment of papers and maps and napkins are tubes and tubes of . . . food. Aluminum food-tubes, dozens of them, the maps and papers only an afterthought. Tubes of olive paste. Lox spread. Chocolate and hazelnut Nutella. Crushed garlic. Crème de Marron. Anchovy paste. Harissa. Umeshiso Japanese sour plum paste. Marzipan.

Some of the tubes are brutally crushed and creased, squeezed from the middle. Some are neatly rolled. Some slit down their bellies and pithed, the edges crusted with dried remains. Some clearly for suckling, their tops encircled with teeth marks.

I turn to the parking P.A.

"Your boss likes to eat paste," I say.

She shakes her head.

"Oh wow," she says. "I think I didn't want to know that."

But I have brightened her evening. Clearly. I leave rewarded, carrying traffic cones, reflective tape—all the tools of her trade. She doesn't care because she's quitting in the morning. To work on her own film, she swears. She wants my address to invite me to the screening.

"I'll probably be dead by then," I say, before I realize how that sounds.

She stiffens, hurt, defensive.

"Thanks a lot," she says. "That is *so* unfair. Indie movies do get made, you know."

"No," I say. "That's not what I meant."

Vaults ◆ Vehicles ◆ Velocity ◆ Venom ◆ Vermiform ◆ Vest ◆ (Crown) Vic
Virgin Voyage ◆ Virtue ◆ Viscous ◆ Visiting ◆ Saint Vitus ◆ Vos glikher, alts beser

V is for Velocity. Speed. *Vos gikher, alts beser*. The faster, the better. What attracts people to speed? I think it is the feeling of getting away with something. I think a human body knows on a cellular level when it is moving too fast to be in control of itself. A body knows it is physics' bitch.

And yet, with the aid of just some added gear—outfits or gizmos, tools, equipment, machines—skis, HEMI engines, hooker headers, bungee cords—a body can control itself, even if it is moving too fast for its own good. Moving too fast for our own good, hurtling through space, thrills us. Inside us, the cells of our body kick into high gear, release substances which allow us to move even faster, take on an enemy of epic proportion such as the laws of motion, physics itself. And these substances, as they flood our bloodstream, and then bathe our brains, give us the illusion of internal speed.

A rush.

All because we are getting away with something. Getting away with something that—on a cellular level—we should not—must not—do. But we do it anyway, don't we? Rob banks and speed away from them in getaway cars. Race performance vehicles on the quarter mile. Jump from planes. Downhill ski. Play locomotive chicken. Take other people's prescription drugs. Have sex with strangers. Or worse, fall in love, a psychosis in its own right.

These things are a rush. Deep inside us, we know we're getting away with something. Our cells are billions of Jiminy Crickets crying out "no, no. You mustn't."

And we chuck those cells under the chin and say, "Sorry, baby. But I gotta. It's the rush. It's the only time I feel truly alive. Free."

Worshippers of the rush, velocity's rush, are courting cellular death. Courting it. And defying it. At least until that one time that they don't—quite.

In plotting my new car's virgin voyage, I am experiencing velocity's rush. I am courting cellular death and my cells are crying out "no, no, you musn't" while at the same time releasing into my bloodstream chemicals which will possibly give me sufficient edge to avoid cellular death—this time.

The chemicals feel good. Feel like I'm getting away with something.

Feeling good feels good. I'd forgotten what it felt like.

But even though I am unmistakably courting cellular death, and am experiencing all the benefits thereto, I am not planning on defying cellular death.

I am planning on getting away with something. But it isn't defying death.

I am planning on escaping. But not with my life.

It's just as well, in a way. Because Velocity makes an even worse god than Reason. Oh, she's kind to her adherents, for a time. At least as long as they've got the goods, the internal machinery, the reflexes and adrenal glands, the gusto and guts. But sooner or later, velocity's children, worshippers of the rush—sooner or later, they squiff out. Get used up. Go down in flames.

And velocity moves on.

Who are these rush-freaks, anyway? Velocity's drag-racer children? Because I know they're not me. Or anyway, weren't.

Well, they're bored kids whose next best prospect is the military. Kids with tremendous physical prowess who can't get comfortable in their own skins. Kids who can't sit still. Kids with some version of what we used to call St. Vitus Dance. Or else they're the children of now-dead rush-freaks who have gotten all sentimental about that parent's death.

Do we start to see a pattern here? Most rush-freaks are children. Well, they'd just about have to be, right? Who else has the reflexes, the stamina, the perfectly functioning adrenal system? And, of course, it doesn't take many years for velocity to use someone up.

Velocity's adherents are a naturally self-limiting pool. Because velocity is powerful, but not more powerful than probability. Or physics. If you keep trying to defy death, sooner or later you'll fail. Speed-freaks eventually squiff out. Speed-freaks tend to die young.

If they didn't, the rush itself would get old. And we can't have that, can we?

For myself, I am enjoying my body's rush. And, barring a miracle, which my faith in reason will not permit, I'll almost certainly die young. But I am not one of velocity's children.

Not really. I am not the kind of person who gets off on speed. I am slow-moving, almost vermiform by nature. Reason's child, not velocity's. I am reason's child, rational and methodical. Even if it means I sometimes crawl. I take my time. I get everything right. I'm not—a leaper.

None of which is to say that I can't handle a 1971 Plymouth Road Runner. I can drive the shit out of a 1971 Plymouth Road Runner. I can drive the birds from the trees. In a 1971 Plymouth Road Runner.

I may crawl. I may creep. I may appear to be moving through something viscous, even when I am going at full power. I may be careful, prudent, scientific in all things.

But I am also a Jersey Girl. And we can drive, man. Especially those of us who traded our virtue for lessons from Eamon "Flattop" O'Leary. We can really drive. That's the thing about us. That's the thing about us, if you were wondering.

V is for Saint Vitus, the patron saint of restless kids and drag-race enthusiasts. Over-sleepers. Comedians. Bored Jersey Girls. And Sicily.

Today, I am a little restless, uncomfortable in my skin, anxious for tomorrow, when Pudge will drive my new muscle car home to me. Once upon a time, because I looked like her, because Timmy loved her, St. Evlalia was my favorite saint. Today, I am considering other applicants. Saint Vitus. Because I'm antsy. And Saint Philip of Neri. For his lovely exit lines ("last of all, we must die"). Today, I am considering other patrons.

Well, patrons to *you*, maybe. After all, these are *still* not my people.

I have no business being antsy, because I still have something essential to take care of. I've been avoiding it, because it's the kind of thing a car would help with. And that gets me thinking about my new car and its virgin voyage. But as I pace the three rooms of my mostly boxed-up apartment, the one I shared with Timmy, the one Timmy leapt from, I somehow summon the focus to get the job done.

I don lipstick and a push-up bra and hail a cab on Howard Street. My real-girl drag and 100 bucks easily persuade the cabbie to help me with the flea tanks and the artificial dog. I am prepared with answers for any question he might have. Sarcastic answers. Enigmatic answers. Intriguing answers.

But the cabdriver in question is sublimely disinterested. His only concerns are traffic (which he loathes with such venom that I cannot believe he is able to function as a cabdriver) and avoiding public housing projects.

Traffic is scant. The Leap is the only thing in Red Hook worth visiting on a Thursday night. And avoiding public housing in a neighborhood that is seventy percent public housing is impossible.

He speeds the cab, a crummy old Crown Vic, past the endless project buildings and I feel it in my body. Warm, like a first shot of whiskey running down the gullet. He is only going fifty, and still I can't stop grinning. No question about it. I have acquired the temporary tutelage of Saint Vitus. Today.

The cabbie helps me into The Leap with the tanks and the artificial dog. We rest them along the back wall. He doffs his cap and leaves. I hear the cab peel out, squealing. Didn't know a Crown Vic *could* peel out, but I guess it's a testament to one man's fear of Red Hook. Or driving prowess. Or bilious horror of possible tunnel traffic. Or too many seventies cop shows. Or something.

The hipsters are immediately intrigued. The boy with no shoes, the one who made the "The Leap" sign, now wearing a furry vest and a wool hat with long, built-in pigtails, leads the charge. He kneels beside the artificial dog. His brethren follow suit. They can hardly believe their eyes. They flag down Boris and order a pitcher of Guinness to drink next to the tanks.

Seeing this, Timmy's fleas entrenched, I'm at ease. Mark is tough. Mark is hard. Mark is squeamish when it comes to anything psychologically sticky. But Mark wants those hipsters. If the customers like the fleas, the fleas will stay.

He is behind the bar, drying glasses and raises a crazy Timmy-eyebrow at me.

"What's this, then?"

I bound up to him.

"Timmy's fleas," I say.

He shakes his head, laughs gently. He chills a stein, dries it, then fills it with Guinness for me. His motions are deliberate, expectant.

"I need you to take care of them for a while."

He sprays the taps and polishes them, wipes the bar.

"Why's that, Iz?"

"Oh, for fuck's sake, Mark. Because I'm going on a trip. Or I'm in the middle of a love affair. Or I'm having a church supper and don't want so many bugs around. Fill in the goddamn blank."

He laughs, vaults over the bar to bring the hipsters a fresh pitcher. They are still crowded around the tanks. Mark comes back around, puts his forearms across the bar to squeeze me.

"I haven't done it since . . . for years, it must be . . . since Timmy was away at sea."

His voice chokes off.

"Well, I wrote everything down for you."

Mark is smiling at me but tears are running down his stubbly face. I gulp down the beer.

"I'm not sure I'm up to the task, Lass."

"Sure you are, Mark. The first recorded proprietor of a flea circus was named Mark. 'Mark, an Englishman.' In the sixteenth century."

I say "Englishman" and Mark's clouded eyes darken further.

"If I can do it, Mark-o, anyone can. Besides, it looks to me like you might be able to charge for the privilege."

I gesture behind him at the hipsters in the barback mirror. Their ringed noses are pressed up against the glass. Mark looks over my head, grins and folds his arms across his torso. Classic

Irish bartender pose. He's not going to let some *Englishman* show him up.

"Another pint?" he says.

"No thanks, I gotta fly."

"Suit yourself. Only, don't be a stranger."

"No," I say, clamber up on the barstool, kiss his gruff old cheek.

I make for the door and a hand grabs my foot. Coo. I hadn't seen him lying there. I kneel at his head. His breath is putrid — *eau de* cellular death.

"I wish I had your courage, Kid."

"Don't start, you sour old jackass."

"I shoulda done it years ago," he murmurs, his eyes rolling back into their deep ashy sockets.

I touch his face.

"Your wife needs someone to yell at. That's reason enough not to. Anyway, it's not courage that impels me."

"What then?" he coughs and whispers.

"Certainty," I say cheerfully.

"And stupidity?"

"That too."

"I got plenty of that," he says, almost petulant.

"Well, what do you want me to say, Coo? You're almost there, anyway."

"True enough."

He passes out again. There is a chunky string of drool running down each side of his face. They join under his chin like a librarian's glasses.

I stand. Wild head rush.

Rush.

Rush, which I am in. *Vos glikher, alts beser.* The faster, the better.

"Godspeed," I whisper, caressing the old wooden doorframe.

And I am out the door and gone before anyone can ask me just what the hell I mean by that.

23. WALL

Wailed ◆ Wake the Dead ◆ Wall ◆ Wanna ◆ Warmed-up ◆ Watched ◆ Weight ◆ Well-tuned
Wet Enough ◆ What's the Difference ◆ Wheels ◆ Whispered ◆ Whole
Why ◆ Willing ◆ Willow Street ◆ Window Shield ◆ Wisdom ◆ Worm ◆ Worst

W is for Wall. I have not yet addressed the question: why did Timmy kill himself? Or, if I have, if I have asked it every second of every day and long hard night for almost a year; if I have whispered it at the cat, wailed it at God, spelled it out in fleas, carved it into my flesh with broken beer bottles, searched the index of every book I own for it—why, why, why?—if it is the question that informs my very being; if it is the question that has undone me, I nonetheless don't have an answer.

Why did Timmy off himself? A professor of a flea circus, is, by his nature, a person of infinite patience and perseverance. So say all the great flea minds of the past whose memoirs adorn my bedstand. Bertolotto. Heckler. Tomlin. María Fernanda Cardoso. Dr. Thomas Moufet, sixteenth century entomologist, author of *Silkwormes and their Flies* as well as "Little Miss Muffit," which he wrote for his daughter, Patience.

Patience. Patience and Perseverance. A person of infinite patience and perseverance.

Well, you'd have to be, right? To harness a flea? To wait while that flea got its tiny two-volt brain around the idea that leaping—its stock in trade—was no longer an option. To repeat that feat by the hundreds, the thousands? Then to build sets and costumes? To feed the fleas and care for them? The ability to persevere would have to be *your* stock in trade.

Why then did Timmy off himself? Why didn't he persevere? What frightened Miss Muffit away?

Why? Why? Why? The answer is walled away from me. The answer's on the other side of a wall. I can't know it. So, it's almost like I never asked at all. Sort of.

Why ask why when I know it is unanswerable? Let's not and say we did. Or let's, and say we didn't. And let's not ask me, either, while we're at it. Why ask me? How should I know?

Why? Because it is the only course of action that has any vibrancy or texture for me.

Why? Because it is the only available option that provides (the illusion of) life.

Why? Because I can do no other. Because I said so. Because it's time. Just because.

Why? Well, what's the difference? There is no difference. Doing it and not doing it are not identical acts, I'll grant you. Doing it and not doing it are not absolutely equal, it is true; but they are congruent at every point, from every perspective but one. Every perspective but mine.

And my (slight) preference is for doing it. My (slight) choice is for action rather than inaction. My (slight) body against the wall.

W is for wall. Not the metaphoric wall I'm up against, walled in by. Not the imaginary wall behind which lies the answer to all those whys.

W is for the actual wall. The earthberm wall encased in concrete. The twenty-foot wall on top of which is the Garden State Parkway. The Willow Street wall. The wall at the end of the block I grew up on.

Other than the wall, the block I grew up on is nothing special. There is nothing about it, for example, that particularly lends itself to teaching someone how to operate a manual transmission. On the left, facing the wall, there is the Peerless Tube factory. On the right, there are houses, one of which I grew up in. Behind the houses' tiny backyards are other, smaller houses. Behind the house I grew up in lives a union widow and her two grown half-wit children whom my mother dubbed Little Big Head One and Little Big Head Two.

Other than the wall at its ass-end, it is an ordinary street in an ordinary town. It is approximately a quarter of a mile long, with a slight left curve which we always called the dogleg. There is nothing about it that particularly cries out: drive a stick.

But it happened to be the street that the town King of the Motorheads Eamon "Flattop" O'Leary favored for teaching people how to drive stick. Fancy stick. Performance stick.

Serious Stick, as he had tooled into his leather vest.

And, as I say, it happened to be the street I grew up on. I watched a lot people learn how to drive Serious Stick on Willow Street in Bloomfield, New Jersey. And when my time came, I myself learned how to drive Serious Stick on Willow Street. In Bloomfield, New Jersey.

Shifting through the gears on Willow Street is something I have done more times than even I, the math geek, can estimate. Other than the wall, there is nothing special about Willow Street, it is true. No neon sign that screams "Standard." But I always thought that if I had reason and opportunity to show off my stick work, Willow Street would be the place to do it.

Look at it this way, I am the proud owner of a classic American performance vehicle. A 1971 Plymouth Road Runner. Sub-lime green with a black vinyl roof. Hurst four-on-the-floor. A HEMI. A car cool enough to leave the great love of your life for Johnny Thunders in. A dream car. A ride of my dreams. A ride for an angel, appearing to me in my dreams.

Of *course* I've gotta use the car to show off my stick work. First thing. I mean, that's only natural, right? And the Raceway Park dragstrip in Englishtown, New Jersey being closed for the season, Willow Street is where I want to do that. Drive some Serious Stick. Clutch effortlessly through the gears. Show off my driving prowess.

If you like, look at it this way. Tonight, Saturday night, my first night in solo possession of my classic American performance vehicle—a dream car in several senses at once—tonight, I'm going to drive some Serious Stick. On Willow Street, in Bloomfield, New Jersey.

And the wall? The wall at the ass-end of Willow Street in Bloomfield, New Jersey? Look at it this way, the wall is just . . . gravy.

It is already Saturday night as I construct these tepid explanations. The sun has set and my new car (mine!) is parked outside my apartment on Howard Street. Pudge and I have just fucked for the last time; fucked so fast and furious, I'm sure there are peel-out marks on the floor of my vaginal canal. Now he is laughing in his half-sleep.

In a few hours he will catch a plane to Kansas to say goodbye to his family and shortly after that, he will be in Australia directing research on a parasitic worm which is mainly found in the Thorn Forests of Bolivia. In a few hours, he will leave to catch a plane to Kansas, and the car will be, irrevocably, mine.

I am enjoying his company. I enjoy everything now that I've decided I won't have to for much longer. But I am getting restless.

"I need to get presents for my nephews," he mutters. "What's a good present for nephews?"

"How about matches?"

He laughs.

"I'm serious. How about Pep Boys matches?"

He rolls over and looks at me, laughing.

"You mean with the three heads?"

"No. I mean with the three big heads on little stick bodies, so they can poke the matches through. Give the Pep Boys giant, red-tipped dicks."

"I don't think my sister would like that."

"The dicks?"

"Or me giving her children matches."

"What have you given them in the past?"

"Bugs," he says. And laughs his lovely, throaty laugh. "But she asked me not to do that anymore."

"See?" I say. "The woman is impossible to please. Trust me, Pep Boys matches will go over great. How old are these nephews anyway?"

"Ten and twelve."

"Old enough to play safely with matches. And penises, for that matter."

"Why are you pushing this so hard?"

"I want to go to Pep Boys, pick up some safety flares."

"Why didn't you say so," he says, and bounds out of bed.

He has said nothing about my boxed-up apartment, my plans for his car, my plans in general. He laughs with genuine joy, watching my driving like it's a movie, squeezing my left thigh as it pumps the bear-trap clutch, all the way to the Pep Boys. He calls a cab to take him to Newark Airport from the parking lot. We practice lighting matches with one hand until it comes. He gives the Road Runner a last, fond glance, then kisses the top of my head, one hand on the cab door.

"Happy trails," I say.

"Right back atya, Kid."

He laughs hot sweet breath into my ear and he is gone.

And the car is mine.

I will say this for Doctor of Parasitology Edward "Pudge" Goroguchi: to the very end, he was good-humored. Impossibly, preposterously good-humored. Of course, he's an amoral son-of-a-bitch, but that is just my good fortune.

To have met him when I did. To have basked in his good humor while I did. To have received from him the beautiful instrument that I did. And to have gotten all that without having to answer any hard questions. Because he didn't particularly care about the answers, one way or the other.

An amoral son-of-a-bitch, but good-humored. I predict he will go far.

As for me, I head down the Parkway an exit or two, *not* far. Toward Bloomfield. Toward the wall.

I pull onto Willow Street from Prospect Avenue, drive slowly past the first few houses and park in front of the house I grew up in. The car is very loud, and very pretty. Such people as I pass point and stare, but it is quite late. Sunday morning, technically. And this is New Jersey, where assertive cars are part of the landscape. I have really garnered hardly any attention at all, considering.

In my mind, I am replaying everything Eamon "Flattop" O'Leary taught me. Trying to remember all his wisdom. Not that I can't drive Serious Stick. But he taught me in a 1991 Honda Civic. Much of his pedagogy came in the form of sentences like "now, if you were driving a *real* car . . ."

Now, I am driving a real car. And I am trying to remember all I was taught. The car is fairly warmed-up from its drive down the highway. *Fairly* warmed-up. She is willing. But not *ready*. If she were a girl you wanted to fuck, he'd say she was wet enough to screw easy, but not wet enough to *get off*. A crude metaphor, I know. But Flattop's expertise was muscle cars, not poetry. Not even the poetry of muscle cars. Just driving them, well and fast, fixing them, souping them up.

Anyhow, she's almost there. A car like mine, properly tuned, wants to *go*. It doesn't take much. And my car is very well-tuned. I can almost see Flattop's approving smile. Ideally, he'd have tweaked her some, probably. Cheater slicks. Hooker Headers between the carburetor and the exhaust, eight pipes of twisted metal intestine. But that's *his* bag, right? Flattop's?

I'm not a seventeen year-old Jersey Boy or a rush-freak or a motorhead. Or even a poet. I'm a creature of reason. Ockham's razor tells me that any of these embellishments would be over-determined. And my heart tells me that waiting to install them would be treason. My car is good enough.

But not—quite—warm enough.

I pump the gas twice to make sure that the automatic choke is closed. Depress the clutch with my left foot, put my right foot on the brake. I turn the ignition key, slide my right foot to the gas. The engine noise impresses even me. Throaty gurgles like Pudge's laugh. Throaty deep gurgle growls—at a decibel level to wake the dead. Or at least usher them on their way.

Flattop liked to use the whole block, always made me start by backing down to Prospect Avenue. I release the parking brake, push the gear lever into reverse. Let the clutch out, give it a little gas.

The gear ratio is very low in reverse, I hear Flattop intone. You don't need much gas.

But trying to listen, to recall Flattop's tutelage over the ground-shaking, bone-quaking roar of my car is a distraction.

The car stalls.

I stall out. Me. I have let the clutch out too fast, trying to hear someone who isn't there. The weight of the entire car against the pressure plate of the clutch is too great to allow the engine to keep spinning. The engine stops dead in mid-stroke.

Enough of Eamon "Flattop" O'Leary. Later for that dude.

His mom was a drunk, anyway.

I push the clutch in, turn the key. Gas while letting the clutch out. Out of reverse, into a forward gear. Foot on brake. Clutch out. Gas. I drive slowly, preternaturally. Fifteen miles per hour. Just past my old house, the tachometer at 3000 mph, I switch to second, drive right up to John F. Kennedy Boulevard, the cross street just before the wall. JFK Boulevard is an off-ramp for the Garden State Parkway.

I can't imagine that anyone would be exiting right about now, but you never know. Maybe Little Big Head Two, coming home from a mixer at the Nitwit center. I park, jump out, haul the traffic cones and safety flares from the back. Space them out, alternating, midway up the exit ramp, far enough from Willow Street, and anything dangerous that might come barreling down it in the middle of this fine Saturday night, that any driver, even a drunken half-wit, could safely stop.

I set the flares off using Pep Boys matches. The sulfur and magnesium smell good. Then, before I know it, I am back in the car, driving slowly around the block, warming her up. I turn back onto Willow Street, position the car in the center—and again, Flattop's voice begins to plague me.

"Of course, if you were driving a *real* car, you'd wanna spin the tires now. Warm 'em up. Softer rubber, better traction," his ghostly voice intones.

And in recalling it, I know I must. Clutch in. Foot on brake. Neutral. First. Clutch still in, no contact between engine and transmission. Depress gas, watch tachometer. 3500 rpm. Let up on the clutch, fast and steady. The back tires spin because they're turning way too fast for the tires to grip. The engine is still accelerating toward the redline.

The tires start to smoke. Crazy blue billows. The screechy sound is shocking, a million dying owls. I can't believe I haven't wakened the whole neighborhood. But if they're awake, they're used to loud noise and stink. No one comes to investigate. I have smoked off a sixteenth of an inch of rubber, easy. 1.3 seconds have passed.

Beautiful.

Ah, Flattop. Where are ye now?

Clutch in. Step on brake. Right foot to gas, 2200 rpm. Let up on clutch. As it engages, I press down harder on the gas. I feel myself pushed against the car, imagine Flattop doing the pushing. This takes 3 seconds, more or less. 5000 rpm.

Clutch in, foot off gas, pull back into second gear. Push foot back on gas, let clutch out. Hear Flattop yell "PUSH!" The car leaps forward and I am at the dogleg.

I think left, lean left, my hands follow suit, fighting the power of the back wheels against the front of the car which is turning even as I think left. 7 seconds. Just past the dogleg.

Clutch in, foot off gas. Hand forward and to the right, through the gate into third. Clutch out. Slam on gas. Wall ahead. 10 seconds have passed. Clutch in, foot off gas.

Fourth gear, straight back from the third. And in the moment before I die, I feel the rush. And I feel alive. It's stupid, right? Unreasonable. Reason would have it that the dead feel dead, don't feel anything. But reason, apparently, doesn't hold sway here.

I know what will happen. The engine block, a solid hunk of iron, will not penetrate the concrete. The whole rest of the car will fold up like an accordion. The back wheels will lift up off the ground. The glass will explode into thousands of chunks. I will be met with a sternum-crushing steering column as the engine block enters the passenger compartment, just as my face, my upper body, still fueled by fourth-gear momentum, flies through the window shield, into the Willow Street wall.

My skull will explode. Melon meets baseball bat. The air

will be filled with a fine pink vapor made up of liquid me. Likely as not, the drive shaft, a metal tube connected to the engine, will snap off at the back universal joint and penetrate the gas tank, a pressed steel vessel, hung between the rear springs, just behind the differential. Likely as not, the drive shaft will penetrate the gas tank. The gas will catch a spark and there will be an immediate explosion.

Likely as not. Hopefully. If luck will have it. A fire will cover a multitude of sins. Spare Little Big Head One the worst of the death of me.

12, now 13, seconds have passed. I know what will happen. Likely as not. If luck will have it. The Staties on the scene—I can already hear their siren music—will know by the cones this was a deliberate act. They will not mourn me. But they might mourn my ride, might say something like, "Oh man, I seen that car last week!"

It's stupid, right? I know what will happen, but still I feel alive. If you're capable of feeling alive, you ought to choose life. It only stands to reason. (Let clutch out, slam on gas, hear Flattop yell "PUSH!") But how could I?

How could I choose life, when reason, sweet reason, was my skin?

Fin

Acknowledgments

Every novel has a fantastically long list of people without whom it wouldn't be. (Mine follows, and it's a doozy.) This novel, however, also has three people without whom it wouldn't be a novel—because it would be true. They are: Rachel Herschman, Dr. Lois Kennedy, and Diane Fried Rothschild.

And next I must thank Maddalena Polletta who published my first book. Her continued belief in me is my secret weapon.

To my mother, I owe more than thanks in a book, but she really, really liked thanks in a book—especially when they said what is still true: "To Joyce Engelson, the smartest girl in town." Not much chance of anyone unseating her this century. I miss her.

Norman Keifetz has been an extraordinary source of support throughout these strange times. Because of him, my daughter gets to see us labor for art's glories as well as for the drudgeries of commerce. No small thing in the midst of a global Despond and we are deeply grateful.

The squares have The Boss, and may they bless and keep each other. But I got my Jersey from a purer strain: my cousin Laura Israel, Chris Johnson and Bill Skiff.

At some point in my twelve-year Odyssey with this book, I probably crashed on your couch. But I crashed longest and hardest with Penny Pattison, Geek Owens, Molly Babe Pattison-Owens and Iggy the Cat.

David Tompkins has really read this book an awful lot of times, and very bravely. Very bravely. No foolin'. Under sort of impossible circumstances. I don't think this can be overstated, and I am profoundly in his debt. Or maybe we're even by now. But still.

To Francine Prose, who rescued it from the scrap heap—and to Tom Devlin and Jay Brida who tried to—I am also indebted.

To Morgan Meis, the keeper of all the knowledge I need, I hereby claim before all creation that if I can but sell enough copies of this thing, I will happily pay him to lay some more of that knowledge on me.

For help with research, cars, surgery, childbirth, sled-dog wrangling, transportation, boxing form, gambling, emergency airline tickets, Chope-watching, Mets-consolation, last-minute elopement, math, succor, shelter, overnight international deliveries, devil box companionship, maternity clothes, translation, driving lessons and curiously calming late nights at the now long-defunct Skala, I also want to thank the following people (this list is absurd, but bear in mind that it was a restless dozen years for me):

Tülin Açıkalın, John Alex, Chris Anthes, Emily Bank, Jane and Elliot and Zack Barowitz, John and Paul Battis, Warner Belanger, James Bell, Chris Beneke, Max Benjamin, Isidore Berlin, Ross Bingham, Dr. Stephanie Blank, Benjamin Blackburn, Donna Blicharz, D.L. Bowman, Brendan Brogan, Gwen Brown, Bob

Burns, Mary Martha and Sandy Campbell, Georgia and Hanna Campbell-Irwin, Jeff Cashen, Anne Champion, Chope, Aaron Cometbus, Jim Coppola, Brooke Corey, Chris and Kate and Robyn and Shay Cornyn, Chris Crachiolo, Kim Anthony Davis, Gia Davis, Kyle Davis, Bernadette Deamico, Dante and Pedro Diez, Cecile Doo-Kingue, Brad Edwards, Karin Elicone, Katya Epstein, Anne Flueckiger, Joshua Rothschild Fried, Lijah Friedman, Sean and Christy Fuller, Joe Gallagher, Daupo Gassaway, Amy and Angel Gawthrop, Josh Gibbs, Steve Gohl, Zagnut Goldenberg, Claudia and Eve Gonson, George, Sr. and Karen Grella, Mike Guetta, Annika Gustafson, Sirianna Jandaly Gustafson, Kim Hagerich, Lisa Hale, Shafer Hall, Sarah Hanley, Mike Harte, Paul Helliwell, John Henderson, Erik and Jasper and Rebekka and River Henriksen, Rebecca Hill, Geoffrey Hollander, Blake Irwin, Phil Jandaly, Beth Jacobson, Sadakat Kadri, Denise Katz, John Kerrigan, Heather Klugh, Sarah Kresh, Brom and Julian "J-Mouse" Keifetz, Darius Knight, Keely Kolmes, Dasavani Lear, Mark Lepage, Ali Liebegott, Jessica Lowery, Dana Lyn, Erica Lyon, Niall and Yvonne McDevitt, Falisha Mamdani, Emily and Kevin Mandel, Tonino Miano, Jed Miller, Howard Mittelmark, Paul Moss, John Murray, Dr. George Mussalli, Kevin Murphy, Tim Murphy, Fiona Niesewand, Julia and Robert and Rónán O'Connell, Eamon O'Leary, Allison Defrees Ouvry, Laura Paul, Jo and Laura Phillips, Dustin and Kit Poms, Rich Pontius, Charles Puckette, Dante Quaglione, Thom Richardson, Sasha Rodriguez, Nancy Romano, Brahm Rosensweig, Mark and Milo Salisbury, Tim Savage, Elanor and Sarah Schoomer, Greta Schwerner, Garrett Scott, Ally Shaw, Steve Simon, Sam Spake, Ruby Stein, Ned O'Leary Steves, Jacque and Bill Suggs, Spike Taylor, Troy Tecau, Jeff, Jerry, Mark, Mary and Steven Tompkins, Lynne Trepanier, Chris Tsakis, Michal Tziyon, Kumiko Uchida, Curt Wasson, John Bunny Welch, Greg Wilcox, Calvin Williamson,

Susan Willmarth, Ron Woo, Dr. Jacqueline Worth, Sarah Wright and Michael Zaidan.

And finally I must thank the dedicated staff at New Issues, and at AWP; and Brendan Lehane whose book *The Compleat Flea* was a touchstone and bedside necessity for this work.

AWP Award Series in the Novel

2010   *Flea Circus: a brief bestiary of grief*
        Mandy Keifetz
        Francine Prose, Judge

2009   *Merit Badges*
        Kevin Fenton
        Jim Shepard, Judge

2008   *Toads' Museum of Freaks and Wonders*
        Goldie Goldbloom
        Joanna Scott, Judge

2007   *We Agreed to Meet Just Here*
        Scott Blackwood
        Robert Eversz, Judge

2006   *The Truth*
        Geoff Rips
        Nicholas Delbanco, Judge

2005   *One Tribe*
        M. Evelina Galang
        Elizabeth McCracken, Judge

Photo by John Bunny Welch

Mandy Keifetz is a 4th-generation New Yorker. Her work has appeared in *.Cent, Penthouse, Vogue, The Review of Contemporary Fiction,* and other 'zines too numerous to count. Her first novel, *Corrido*, has been optioned by a UK production company. She was a Fellow with the New York Foundation for the Arts in 2002 and her plays have been staged in New York, London, Cambridge, Montréal, and Oslo. She is an occasional MFA dissertation defense panelist at U-MASS, Amherst. She lives in Brooklyn with an opera composer, their child, and an exuberant hound dog.